HOW TO FIND FREEDOM AND KILL YOUR FEAR

THE HEROIC LIFE STORY OF MALCOLM X (MALCOLM X BIOGRAPHY)

JEFFREY JORDAN

© Copyright 2020 - All rights reserved.

The content contained within this book may not be reproduced, duplicated or transmitted without direct written permission from the author or the publisher.

Under no circumstances will any blame or legal responsibility be held against the publisher, or author, for any damages, reparation, or monetary loss due to the information contained within this book, either directly or indirectly.

LEGAL NOTICE

This book is copyright protected. It is only for personal use. You cannot amend, distribute, sell, use, quote or paraphrase any part, or the content within this book, without the consent of the author or publisher.

DISCLAIMER NOTICE

Please note the information contained within this document is for educational and entertainment purposes only. All effort has been executed to present accurate, up to date, reliable, complete information. No warranties of any kind are declared or implied. Readers acknowledge that the author is not engaged in the rendering of legal, financial, medical or professional advice. The content within this book has been derived from various sources. Please consult a licensed professional before attempting any techniques outlined in this book.

By reading this document, the reader agrees that under no circumstances is the author responsible for any losses, direct or indirect, that are incurred as a result of the use of the information contained within this document, including, but not limited to, errors, omissions, or inaccuracies.

CONTENTS

Introduction	ix
Chapter 1: Childhood and Youth	1
Chapter 2: Prison	11
Chapter 3: Family	23
Chapter 4: Nation of Islam	31
Chapter 5: The Hajj Travel and Spiritual Transformation	41
Chapter 6: Struggle for Civil Rights	53
Chapter 7: Martin Luther King	63
Chapter 8: Muhammad Alli	75
Chapter 9: Black Panthers	85
Chapter 10: Views and Transformation	97
Chapter 11: Murder	107
Chapter 12: Legacy	117
Conclusion	127
Help Other Readers to Discover This Book	133
References	135

INTRODUCTION

"Don't be in a hurry to condemn because he doesn't do what you do or think as you think or as fast. There was a time when you didn't know what you know today."

— MALCOLM X

Who was Malcolm X? If you asked your grandparents, they might have labeled him as an African American civil rights activist. If you asked a Baby Boomer, they might tell you that he was a rebel. If you asked someone from Generation X, they might give you a more complex answer. They might say that Malcolm X fought the discrimination of African Americans and paved the path for his fellow Black Americans to rise up and begin fighting for their human and civil rights. He also advocated for the defense of those rights "by any means necessary," and his speeches were often infused with anger toward the dominating White society. At the same time, he championed a fierce desire for his kin to rise above poverty and assume their rightful place in society. Either way, Malcolm X remains one of the most prominent figures of the mid-20th century US political scene, and his legacy is that of a charismatic leader who empowered everyone who heard him speak. Although his work aimed strictly at African Americans, he has the respect of people of all colors, ethnicities, and nations worldwide. Some would say that he was a Black supremacist, and others consider him a peacemaker. So, who was Malcolm X?

Malcolm X was one of the fiercest African American rights activists. Like the majority of Black leaders of the mid-20th century, Malcolm experienced his own share of pain and suffering. His family was virtually destroyed by systematic racism of the time, despite the tolerant, pacifist narratives that had emerged in the mainstream media and politics long before. Malcolm lived in a country that took pride in its wealth and a strong sense of justice. He lived in the proud, democratic United States. But, as you're about to learn, he made sure that the public knew that the dream they were fed was nothing but a smokescreen. For behind the curtain of prosperity and justice laid a world of the rejected, isolated, humiliated, and those left to fend for themselves in a world that saw them barely as human beings. All of this was due to the color of their skin. The reality of the 1930s, '40s, '50s, and '60s in America was grim for African Americans.

Malcolm, like many of Black Americans, saw crime as the only way to survive. He fell victim to addiction and vice, and he found the light only after being imprisoned.

Fast forward some 80 or 90 years, and the Black community in the early 21st century faces almost the same issues as they did a century ago. The legacy of Malcolm X assures that pain and suffering aren't forgotten, and more importantly, it gives hope to rise above all challenges.

In this book, you will learn about who Malcolm X was, and how he came to build the philosophy he had lived. You will learn how Malcolm X, once named Malcolm Little, rose above growing up in poverty, his family being persecuted by the Ku Klux Klan, his father murdered, and his mother broken by the social injustices. You will learn how Malcolm overcame anger, pain, and addiction to gain the purpose and discipline needed for success in life.

In this book, you will also learn how Malcolm X became one of America's most prominent leaders. You will learn how he addressed social injustices and empowered people to take action instead of suffering oppression in silence. You will learn how Malcolm found support in the Nation of Islam, an organization that had a controversial reputation, but most certainly had helped thousands of ex-convicts to recover from addiction and live a stand-up life. You will learn how Malcolm grew his influence within this organization, and how staying true to himself and open to change helped him grow.

In this book, you'll read about how Malcolm X rose to the highest ranks of the Nation of Islam, what his activities and work looked like, and more importantly, how he drew from his and others' life experiences to form empowering philosophy.

In this book, you will also learn about the dangers of ruffling the feathers of a society that was set in its ways, unwilling to look past its own injustices, and admit the need for a change. You will learn how and why Malcolm X was seen as dangerous, and how his honest nature and drive for growth, combined with his fiery temper, eventually led to his downfall.

In this book, you'll also learn how Malcolm's views on society grew, developed, and changed. You'll learn how and why he became a Black nationalist, and which experiences and events led him to embrace the ideas of universal freedom, peace, and equality.

In this book, you'll also learn how Malcolm made connections with celebrities like Muhammad Ali, how he managed to see and spark the best in people, and how he inspired other individuals to form organizations that fought for Black civil rights and equality.

In this book, you will also learn about how Malcolm X died, and get a deeper look at the mysteries surrounding his murder. This will help you understand the events that took place "behind the scenes," even without the knowledge of Malcolm himself. You will learn what caused him to make enemies of people who were once friends, why the media discredited as much as they did, and who was truly behind the attack on his life.

CHAPTER 1: CHILDHOOD AND YOUTH

Malcolm's family faced challenges even before he was born. His father, a Baptist minister, was targeted by the Ku Klux Klan. The first incident the family faced happened in his home in Omaha, Nebraska when armed riders came to their doorstep and threatened them into leaving town, after which they shattered the windows of their house. They accused his father of spreading trouble with his teachings. Malcolm's father was a member of UNIA, an organization that advocated for African Americans to return to Africa and nurture their roots. Upon hearing about this incident, Malcolm's father decided that the family would move once he was born (X., 2015).

Early Persecution and Tragedy

Malcolm's father believed that African Americans couldn't achieve self-respect, freedom, and independence in America. His views made him a controversial figure, and his appearance matched his fierce reputation. As stated in Malcolm X's autobiography, his father had only one eye, and it was unknown how he lost his other eye. He was a tall, strong man, who grew up in Reynolds, Georgia. Malcolm's father faced discrimination and loss since early childhood. He witnessed four of his brothers being murder by White people, and one of his brothers lost his life to lynching.

Malcolm had seven brothers and sisters, three of whom were from his father's previous marriage. In his autobiography, Malcolm states that his mother, Louise Little, was half-White and that she was born as a result of a sexual assault. His origin affected his appearance, giving him lighter skin and a reddish tone to his hair. His mother also had a lighter complexion and distinctly straight hair. At the time when Malcolm was a young adult, lighter complexion in African Americans was viewed as a sort of a status symbol, which he felt and later came to regret.

Malcolm's father followed Marcus Garvey's teachings that advocated African Americans being independent of the White people, which is why he was committed to building his own business and raising his own food. As a part of this concept, he preached in local African American Baptist churches, first in Milwaukee and then in Lansing, Michigan. His views and preachings caused outrage among local hate societies wherever the family went. The next incident happened after Malcolm's father voiced his intentions to open a store, which sparked rage over an African American wanting to own a business and live outside the Lansing district. This ambition came across as "spreading unrest" among other African Americans. After Malcolm's youngest sister was born in 1929, his home was set on fire. The family escaped the fire, and the authorities, although arriving at the scene soon after, couldn't do anything to prevent the home from being completely destroyed.

After the attack on his family, Malcolm, with his parents and siblings, moved to the border of East Lansing. African Americans weren't allowed to be on the streets at night in this area, which would later become the location where Malcolm held one of his University speeches in 1963. The family soon moved again because of harassment, this time out of town where his father built a large house on his own. Harassment followed still, and this time by the police. In his autobiography, Malcolm remembers frequent visits by the police who requested to search the property and inquired about the weapon that his father used to defend the family from their attackers.

Violence didn't only plague Malcolm's family from the outside. He recalls domestic violence as well, as his father would occasionally strike his mother during arguments. His father was strict and wouldn't tolerate his children breaking rules, and would frequently punish them for it.

Life in Poverty

Malcolm learned early on that being Black in society created many paradoxes. He was half-white, which meant that he would never be fully accepted neither by the Black nor the White community. He started working as a young boy, when he hunted and shot animals, recalling that he felt that people were buying them as a courtesy to him and his brother rather than from a need for the food. He also worked as a dishwasher, but his family still struggled to make ends meet. Both he and his mother were a little bit better accepted since they were lighter skinned, but his mother would frequently lose jobs once her employers learned that she was White. He also experienced a lot of cruelty, with White boys trying to talk him into approaching White girls, in which case he could be lynched if he touched them. He experienced some early high school success, becoming the first-ranked student in the class, and eventually the class president. However, much of this success is considered to be as a result of the school's effort to cover their racism. Here, Malcolm realizes that he will be allowed success only until the point where he doesn't disturb the dynamics and order of the White society too much.

He observed that he was doing a little bit better compared to the majority of Black children, but the lion's share could be attributed to his lighter tone. He felt like society was treating him like a harmless, yet expendable novelty, without seeing him as a person with a personality and goals. This led to him feeling emasculated and denied independence and power that most men need. This can be linked with his later obsession with reputation. Instead of feeling accepted for who he was, Malcolm felt like society was parading lighter skinned Black people as an example of how African Americans should look and behave.

Crime and Brushes With the Law

Malcolm, 16, moved to Boston, and after exploring the city for a while, found a job. There, he noticed the difference between how middle-class African Americans lived and the struggles of people living in the ghetto. Malcolm was thrown off by the lifestyle and mannerisms of middle-class African Americans, and he was more drawn to the ghetto environment. He started working in a pool hall when he met Shorty, his future closest friend. Shorty played the saxophone and had connections around the city, which helped in arranging the first job for Malcolm. He started working as a shoeshine boy, which didn't earn him a lot of money. However, Malcolm later found out that the majority of profit from this job came from carrying drugs between dealers and customers. Soon, Malcolm began drinking, gambling, using drugs, and smoking. He changed his style and began wearing fashionable outfits. He was a passionate dancer and had overcome his shyness. His lifestyle now consisted of dealing drugs, nightlife, and dancing.

After quitting his job as the shoeshine boy, Malcolm started working as a drugstore clerk. He didn't enjoy the atmosphere of the middle-class environment, but still bonded and developed a friendship with a patron, a high school student named Laura. Malcolm and Laura enjoyed dancing, but he soon met Sophia, another woman with whom he bonded. Sophia dated multiple White men aside from Malcolm, and his sister disapproved of the relationship. This relationship drove a wedge between Malcolm and his sister, and he later moved in with his friend Shorty. During this period, Malcolm recognized some hypocrisy in the way Roxbury African Americans judged one another based on material possessions, looks, and other things, comparing it with how the rest of the society was looking at them. Malcolm recognized that the lifestyle of the Roxbury Hill folk was filled with self-defacement and that the group had lost its identity in the effort to mimic White people. He best depicted this in describing the act of conking one's hair, which consists of applying chemicals to straighten it. Malcolm sees this as the ultimate symbol of a US African giving up on their authenticity by altering one of the most recognizable race features—their hair—to fit the beauty ideal that was set by the White society. In a way, his relationship with Sophia was a way for Malcolm to get revenge for how he was treated as a boy—as a status symbol that wasn't viewed as a real human being.

Soon after this, Malcolm found a job at a Boston–Washington train line and the Boston–New York train line, where he sold sandwiches.

He is again drawn by the city's nightlife and wealth but

gets fired for being too aggressive about selling sandwiches. Malcolm enjoyed his next job much more, as a waiter in Harlem's Small's Paradise bar. There Malcolm learned the underground ways and etiquette, and mastered a few more hustling techniques. He also learned about famous gangsters of the time, and in the 1930s, became close to a man called Sammy the Pimp. Sammy quickly became his best friend, and Malcolm moved into a rooming house, where he met a number of female prostitutes. He used his time at this housing to learn about the psychology of the men the prostitutes were meeting and he became friends with numerous women. Despite learning a lot in his new setting, Malcolm eventually lost his job at the bar after he referred an undercover military agent to a prostitute. This is when he started selling marijuana with the help of his trusted friend, Sammy the Pimp.

The work was lucrative for him at first, but Malcolm soon began moving frequently to avoid the police, and such a lifestyle was costly. To make the matter worse, Malcolm soon became addicted to marijuana and frequently had to borrow money for basic expenses, like food. After a short visit to Boston to see his friend Shorty, Malcolm further got into trouble for an armed conflict with a fellow gambler. The environment wasn't safe for him to deal drugs, so he began doing a series of robberies which led to gun running. He also renewed his romance with his ex-flame Sophia, this time discreetly, since she was married. The lifestyle soon took a further toll on Malcolm, who began using harder drugs like cocaine to deal with the stress of trafficking guns.

The stress on Malcolm further increased with the changing climate in Harlem. The effects of World War II increased tensions between races, and the public began viewing White women socializing with Black men and dancing in bars more unfavorably. Police raids became more frequent, and the Savoy Ballroom, a place where Malcolm frequently dwelled, got shut down. The nightlife became a lot less profitable, and the surrounding tension drove a wedge between Malcolm and Sammy, culminating in Sammy threatening Malcolm with a gun after an argument. The two friends eventually made up, but the trust was never fully regained. During this time, Malcolm rented an apartment with his brother Reginald. The two brothers' connection strengthened during this time of tension, and Malcolm began relying more and more on his brother. These experiences further deepened Malcolm's intolerance toward White people, whom he blamed for the conditions his people were living in. Malcolm does take some accountability for his actions and places some on his Black community, but overall he observed the social climate they were living in as the primary contributor to thriving crime, poverty, and moral decay. Torn between the obvious depravity present in the ghetto and his contempt for the middle-class Black community, Malcolm began to feel like Black people just couldn't win. This further angered him, and he felt like living a hustler's life was his only option for self-preservation. Although he hadn't yet gone through a life-changing transformation, this was when Malcolm began to feel like African Americans needed a more empowering attitude to get ahead in life.

However, a series of conflicts that culminated in Malcolm being hunted by the police drove him out of Harlem and back to Boston. Although he stayed with his sister Ella, his relationship with Sofia intensified since her husband was traveling frequently. Malcolm formed a group with two more men, Sofia, and her younger sister for the purpose of doing robberies. The women would present themselves as saleswomen to be let in the house for a tour, later informing the men of the home's layout. The group performed several robberies, but these weren't what ultimately led to Malcolm's arrest. Malcolm was hunted and eventually arrested by the police when he exposed his intimate relationship with Sophia in front of her husband's friend. In his autobiography, Malcolm recalls being questioned more about his relationship with White women than about the crimes he had committed. He willingly surrendered to the police, which was later seen as his first step toward transformation, and eventually he was sentenced to ten years in prison. As we all know, that was when the true adventures in his life began.

CHAPTER 2: PRISON

The journey through his prison sentence shaped many of Malcolm's beliefs and actions that remained as a legacy after his passing. This journey began when he was still suffering from drug withdrawal, and the combination of this crisis with his naturally fierce temper resulted in him being placed into solitary confinement. In prison, his nickname was 'Satan'. However, this was about to change when Malcolm met Bimbi, a Black prisoner whose views differentiated him from the crowd. Bimbi advocated for mutual respect between inmates and guards, and mutual respect among the prisoners. This teaching motivated Malcolm to abandon his rebellious beliefs and start nurturing a more intellectual, peaceful mindset (Goldman, 1979).

. . .

Studies in Prison

Soon after being sentenced, Malcolm began reading in the prison library. Over time, his language skills improved, but more importantly, his beliefs and behavior began to change. He started mastering the art of reasoned argumentation instead of responding with rage and conflict. This gradual change resulted in Malcolm being moved to Norfolk Prison Colony in 1948. This facility offered a better education environment for inmates and was less violent overall. It had a robust library, where inmates were able to study a broad choice of subjects related to linguistics, literature, biology, and religion.

This was when Malcolm first learned about the existence of the Nation of Islam. If you recall, his family, and his mother in particular, were prone to making dietary choices based on religious beliefs and giving up pork was discussed in his early childhood. When Malcolm connected with his brother Reginald, he started making the first steps toward joining the Nation of Islam. Right around this time, Malcolm encountered the beliefs about White men's innate wickedness, which aligned with the experiences Malcolm had throughout his life.

Malcolm Little began serving his prison sentence in 1946 when he was only 20 years old. He found an intellectual and spiritual escape in reading and learning upon joining the community of Black Muslims. Some of his thoughts during this period suggest that he found a sense of freedom in learning despite being behind bars. This speaks a lot to his personality, particularly if we ponder upon his statement that he would often forget about being imprisoned while learning. Such inspiration and thirst for knowledge at such a young age can most certainly be attributed to Malcolm's natural potential that he didn't have the ability to show in the past, nor had he been in the right environment. Malcolm claimed that focusing on his studies kept his mind out of prison for months at a time, which inspired his reflections on several important issues:

- A man who used to be involved in what we'd call, some of the most criminal activities (aside from any crimes against the safety of others, to which Malcolm wasn't ever prone), when given proper structure and direction in life, he discovered interests and potentials he never even assumed he had.
- Intellectual stimulation gave Malcolm greater satisfaction than material things, even surpassing the urge and desire for freedom that most people would feel in prison.
- When he was finally given direction and a community he felt like he could trust, and particularly with the appearance of a leading male figure in his life, Malcolm was quick to abandon his once hedonistic lifestyle and accepted a quite strict set of life principles that

were the complete opposite to those he used to live by.

Not only had Malcolm lost interest in gambling, drugs, and hustle, but he also put a lot of effort into learning. He learned out of his own desire, even staying up after the lights were out, when he'd read on the floor of his cell with only the light of the corridor bulb shining upon him. This shows that he was now willing to make sacrifices for self-improvement, and had made one of the most difficult, albeit most beneficial changes a human can make. He started deriving a sense of pleasure and fulfillment out of activities that are otherwise boring and tiresome to most people, like exercise and studying. Of course, there are many who enjoy these activities, but people who are in the direst need of change often can't get themselves to change negative behaviors, like drinking and overeating. The reason for that is that their minds are set in their ways, only capable of deriving pleasure from doing these harmful activities. To make a change such as Malcolm's requires a grand capacity of self-control and a lot of determination. We can also reflect on the fact that Malcolm most likely had these abilities all along but was simply in a social setting that didn't support him in any way.

Some of Malcolm's earliest experiences may have instilled many self-defeating beliefs, but it was his time in prison that made him question these beliefs. At first, Malcolm witnessed being both favored and detested for his skin color within his own family, with his mother rejecting him over his lighter skin, and his father favoring him. Despite the tragic loss of his father, he also recalled having mixed feelings toward him, and the relationship between the two of them was far from what we'd consider desirable, nowadays, to support the personal growth and development of a young man (or a woman for that matter). From what we know about how early parent-child relationships shape a human being, we can deduce that Malcolm was discouraged very early on, and by two figures he admired and respected despite the scoldings and beatings he suffered. Today, we know that growing up in a setting like this is exactly what puts young people on the path of crime. A combination of poverty, a shunned life in a racially segregated community, the persecution that his family suffered for advocating civil rights, and ultimately the murder of his father as a culmination of the harassment the family suffered, could have installed a set of such defeating beliefs into a young boy that only a complete separation from his former life could untangle. It's important to note that, for a person to change, they must first question everything they believe about the world. In Malcolm's case, prison did exactly what it was meant to do, and it is to rehabilitate. However, the willingness and openness to questioning one's perception of reality were Malcolm's alone. We can argue that, if more people had this ability, the world would be a much better place.

Malcolm's natural curiosity and intellectual drive made him fascinated with words he never heard before, and the meanings and history behind these words. He was so immersed in his studies that he would wake up thinking about the words he learned the past night, and was compelled to spend the following day learning more.

Once called 'Satan' for his hatred for religion, God, and the Bible, Malcolm soon made a transformation under the influence of his sisters. Malcolm's sisters wrote to him regularly, telling him about a teacher called Elijah Muhammad. They urged him to embrace Islam as the "Black man's religion". The introduction to Elijah Muhammad's teachings introduced Malcolm to a whole community that felt exactly like him and believed that White people were sent by the devil to torture all non-White people. Being introduced to these teachings might not be considered good by today's standards, but we also need to put these teachings in perspective in order to understand them correctly:

- This era openly and with very little restraint separated races and still believed in Black inferiority, showing very little regard for the life and well-being of non-White people.
- Finally admitting what he most likely felt for a very long time, and being surrounded by people who shared these beliefs, enabled

Malcolm to start growing a sense of dignity and let go of self-hatred he often felt for being Black.

The complexity of racial relations and identities of the era requires careful consideration before forming any conclusions, and we always need to look into the context of the time, analyze people's experiences, and real-life circumstances before making a final judgment. In Malcolm's case, this form of radicalism was the only way to strengthen his self-esteem and identity, and it explains how and why it led to so much improvement. From a modern day perspective, we couldn't say that being a part of a community like this was a good thing, but it was for Malcolm. To Malcolm, becoming a Muslim and being a part of the Nation of Islam meant getting in touch with his origins. It also meant breaking racial stereotypes which, at the time, was close to revolutionary.

Malcolm's persistence in copying the dictionary, reading, and participating in study groups opened a whole new world of understanding for him. It also presented him with an opportunity to get transferred into Norfolk's experimental prison, with his sisters' help. Malcolm persisted in his efforts to keep learning, even if it meant staying up until four in the morning and jumping back into bed each time the guard would pass by his door.

Malcolm's studying during prison wasn't only about gaining knowledge and expanding his vocabulary. He was eager to test his faith against the writings that contained different views on politics, society, and religion. He expressed true intellectual curiosity by reading not only those works that supported his views, but also those that opposed them. He studied DuBois, Herodotus, Gandhi, Socrates, and others, exposing himself to a broad range of contradicting views. This helped him form a profound understanding of his own religion, and ultimately to understand the extent of the damage that poor education was afflicting on African Americans. We now know that education is one of the main factors that determines progress from stagnation and decay, whether moral, wealth, health, or behavioral.

Thirst for Knowledge

Aside from transforming his belief system, Malcolm proceeded to advance his education while in prison. He persisted in his habit of copying words from the dictionary and had copied the entire book. This expanded his vocabulary, prompting him to better his reading skills and habits. In his autobiography, Malcolm states that extensive reading in his cell late into the night awakened his urge for intellectual activity. His reading and studying resulted in him developing a belief system that centered around Africa. He learned that the first civilizations originated in Africa and that some of the most prominent figures from ancient history, like

Egyptian pharaohs, were African. Furthermore, Malcolm began studying anti-British resistance of China and India, where he learned about the truth of colonialism.

Malcolm began public speaking after joining the prison's debate program. His arguments were unique for his ability to add a racial argument to each topic that was being discussed. Being a part of the debate team enabled Malcolm to advance his rhetorical skills, which he later used to convert other inmates to the Nation of Islam. He proceeded to emphasize that Jesus Christ wasn't White and had devoted his time to gaining as much attention as he could. Soon after this, his brother Reginald was suspended from the Nation of Islam. This was a result of his affair with a secretary, which prompted Malcolm to disown him. He believed that his brother was being punished for his sins and continued to try to convert more fellow inmates into Islam. Moreover, he began using a language that depicted the shift in his perception of his past and life in general. He began expressing his beliefs in extremes, using strong opposites like good and bad, black or white. His later thoughts and speeches seem to ignore the presence of White people in his life who had treated him well, like his former boss and foster-parents. Such extreme ways of thinking can be attributed to Malcolm's desire to find moral clarity.

However, he began using more complex language and evolved his views on good and evil, later on, gaining a deeper understanding that there was a spectrum of people who have different characters and attributes. This subtle change signifies the abandonment of earlier simplistic views, and he began recognizing personality traits regardless of skin color. He even stated his realization that his early attitudes on race didn't match all of his experiences.

Release From Prison

Both anti-Black and anti-White attitudes of the time originated out of fear, however, the views that were being preached by the Nation of Islam were outside the social norm. On the other hand, racial and ethnic prejudices against minorities had grown with the fear that minorities would take over jobs, corrupt schools, and increase crime in White communities. In this sense, Malcolm's anti-White prejudice was quite different from the majority of social prejudice of the time. Still, Elijah Muhammad's views were those of a minority of Black people, whereas prejudice of White Americans toward Africans and Asians attracted millions and have plagued both public and private institutions.

Malcolm was released on parole in August 1952 and placed in the custody of Wilfred, one of his brothers. Wilfred was now living in a Muslim household and had created a sense of warmth and order in his homestead. Malcolm was instantly excited about the austerity and solidarity during his first temple meeting with the

Nation of Islam. He was publicly recognized by Elijah Muhammad and compared to Job, the biblical figure, for his newfound faith and strength to resist the temptations of the world after leaving prison. Soon after being released from prison, Malcolm showed interest in recruiting new members and received advice from Elijah Muhammad on how to best reach out to young people.

At the beginning of his work, Malcolm doesn't have a lot of luck with attracting new members to the organization. However, memberships triple throughout the course of the following months. At this time, Malcolm decided to change his last name to X, which expressed his unknown African last name. He began speaking at the Nation's temple meetings, increasing his orator confidence. He was then appointed as assistant minister at the Detroit temple.

CHAPTER 3: FAMILY

Malcolm's family life largely shaped his beliefs and work. Before meeting his future wife, Betty, in 1958, Malcolm practiced celibacy for ten years. Despite being interested in Betty, Malcolm didn't court her directly. Instead, Malcolm first introduced his love interest to Elijah Muhammad, and then proposed in Detroit from a payphone. After getting married, the couple settled in Queens, New York. They had five children, four being born while Malcolm was alive, and his youngest after his passing. Despite initial rejection, Malcolm's sister converted to Islam in 1958 and joined the organization.

Malcolm's brother Reginald first informed him of Elijah Muhammad, who was the Nation of Islam's spiritual leader. His central teachings involved Islamic teachings that inspired Malcolm to reflect on those who conspired against him and hurt him. During these reflections,

Malcolm adopted Islamic teachings. He eventually accepted the principles of the Nation of Islam, which propagated that Black people were the first humans on Earth and that the White race was unleashed as an evil force to enslave the African nations. Therefore, the religion, myths, customs, and names that were adopted by the Black people were a result of enslavement. According to Elijah Muhammad's teachings, the "White civilization" had begun to destroy itself. Upon accepting these teachings, Malcolm proceeded to communicate with Elijah Muhammad and prayed as a part of his religious practice.

Betty Shabazz

Betty Shabazz was one of the most important figures in Malcolm's life. She and Malcolm created a family of many children, and the relationship was known to be caring and respectful. Some of the letters discovered after Malcolm's death suggested he would frequently write to Elijah Muhammad for marriage advice, particularly for how to make his wife happy. Betty Shabazz, born in 1934 as Betty Dean Sanders, spent the majority of her childhood in Detroit. She was exposed to activism in her early teens, after she began living with an activist Helen Malloy and her husband, a businessman Lorenzo Malloy. Hellen Malloy often organized protests against African American discrimination, often in front of stores and other establishments.

After finishing high school, Betty studied at Alabama's Tuskegee Institute. There she encountered severe racism, which was the reason why she left the facility and went on to study at New York City's Brooklyn State college. The racism she encountered there affected her as well, although it was less severe and obvious. Like many African Americans at the time, Betty's experiences compelled her to begin fighting against racism. She first visited the Nation's temple in Harlem at the invitation of an older nurse. While she enjoyed the evening, Betty at first declined to join the Nation. Her friend was a member of Malcolm's temple, and she met him through her the next time she visited the temple. She converted in 1956, after spending some time listening to Malcolm's services. Like Malcolm, she also changed her last name to X, suggesting that she had let go of the surname given to her by enslavers.

Malcolm X and Betty Shabazz had six daughters by 1964, when they left the Nation of Islam. Malcolm and his family then became Sunni Muslims. Betty was presented on the day of the Malcolm's assassination at the New York City's Audubon Ballroom. After Malcolm's death, Betty stated that she heard the gunshots being fired, but didn't realize that Malcolm was the target right away. She got on the floor with her children and was horrified to notice that people were standing in astonishment near the spot where Malcolm had been standing. In a chilling interview, Betty described how she was slowly coming to the realization that Malcolm was gunned down as she was approaching the crowd. She approached the dying Malcolm, who showed signs of life for a couple more seconds. Betty, as well as her daughters, witnessed the last moments of Malcolm's life.

One of Malcolm's assassins was caught and beat up by the angry crowd right after the shooting, which all happened in the presence of Malcolm's family. After losing her husband, Betty Shabazz never remarried. She devoted her life to raising their six daughters. Since Malcolm was the sole provider for the family, his death left the family in a financial crisis. The annual income from the sales of Malcolm's autobiography and other publications helped the family get through these difficult times. Betty graduated from the Jersey City State College in 1969 and earned a PhD in Higher Education Administration from the Massachusetts University. She was offered a position at the Medgar Evers College in New York, which she accepted. Betty worked as an associate professor, an administrator, and a fundraiser for the remainder of her life.

Suspicions surrounding Malcolm's death haunt his family until this day. Betty and his daughters suspected and had openly accused the Nation of either directly or indirectly ordering Malcolm's murder. Louis Farrakhan, the Nation's leader at the time, was accused of instigating Malcolm's assassination. The heaviness of Malcolm's death never allowed the family to move on. Betty's daughter Qubilah Shabazz was prosecuted in

1995 for ordering Farahan's murder. However, this incident took an unexpected turn. Farrakhan defended Qubilah and reached out to Malcolm's family, which resulted in a public reconciliation. Tragedy followed Malcolm's family even after his death. His wife, Betty, died in a fire that was set by her grandson Malcolm, who was 12 years old at the time. Malcolm was Qubilah's son, who had been sent to live with his grandmother after his mother began attending a rehabilitation program. Malcolm Shabazz was sentenced to juvenile detention after the incident, and his grandmother was buried in New York's Hartsdale Cemetery alongside Malcolm.

Malcolm X and Betty Shabazz had six daughters. With the exception of Qubilah, whose life led her to a path of tragedy, his other daughters devoted their lives to human rights activism in order to honor their father's legacy. Attallah, Gamilah, Ilyasah, Malaak, and Malikah Shabaz were very young when they lost their father, and the family faced many challenges both within itself and in the aftermath of their father's murder.

Malcolm Shabazz

After Betty Shabazz's death by the fire he set, Malcolm was put in a juvenile detention facility, where he remained for four more years. After the accident, Malcolm, who was 12 at the time, was described as a brilliant child, yet schizophrenic and psychotic.

Malcolm's life was cut short, as he died in 2013 at the age of 28 after a fight in a bar in Mexico. Malcolm expressed great regret over his grandmother's death, but incidents followed him regardless.

Attallah Shabazz

Malcolm X's oldest daughter found major success in her activism, theatrical, producing, directing, and academic endeavors. In 2002, she was recognized as a minister of Belize by the Honorable Said Musa. As the ambassador-at-large, she represented Belize internationally. Attallah advanced in school from childhood, graduating from the UN International school when she was 17, and earning an international law degree from Briarcliff College. To honor her father's Holy Land journey, Attallah established the Pilgrimage Foundation. This foundation was a way to work toward fulfilling her father's vision of religious oneness.

Gamilah Lumumba Shabazz

Born in 1964, Gamilah was born just a year before her father's passing. Her recent projects involved participating in fashion designs featuring her father's image alongside her sisters. This line was called "Malcolm X Legacy", and features multiple clothing items that display Malcolm's memorable slogans.

. . .

Ilyasah Shabazz

Ilyasah is Malcolm's third daughter, and the most publicly active at the current time. She is a motivational speaker who is devoted to honoring her father's legacy. She is a college lecturer and a children's book author as well. Recently, Ilyasah participated in a documentary that exposed many errors and unknown details about her father's assassination and had participated in many interviews that shed the light on little-known details and circumstances surrounding Malcolm's death. She is devoted to empowering future generations to better understand historic civilizations from multiple angles and is committed to spreading a vision of life in diverse cultures.

Malaak and Malikah Shabazz

Like her sisters, Malaak is also a human rights activist who works to empower people of color worldwide and keep her father's vision alive. She is devoted to fighting for justice across the world and sees her father's death as a grave loss for the idea of human rights itself. Unlike her twin sister Malaak, Malikah Shabazz had numerous brushes with the law and has a history of feuding with her sisters. In 2017, pitbulls were discovered on her estate in such poor conditions that she was accused of animal cruelty.

The family's efforts to keep doing Malcolm's work and

never stop accusing those who they felt were responsible for his death were valuable for many reasons. It has been said that, since his work and vision lived on, those who wished to silence Malcolm failed despite succeeding in killing him. The work of a single man has now been multiplied, and the family's prevailing efforts to find justice for the tragedy eventually led to many astonishing pieces of information reaching the public. More importantly, Malcolm's wife and daughters made sure that his legacy lives on, proving that all allegations against their father were false.

CHAPTER 4: NATION OF ISLAM

Soon after being appointed to his new position, Malcolm learned the life story of his mentor. Elijah Muhammad was born in 1897, in Georgia. He advocated a non-confrontational, yet still open and frank relationship with White people, mainly his employers. He converted to Islam under the influence of Wallace D. Fard, who was a self-proclaimed prophet. Fard's life story ended on a tragic note, with his disappearance. After the loss of his mentor, Elijah Muhammad suffered a similar persecution to that of Malcolm's father. He faced death threats and vicious rivalry for spreading his teachings, which forced him to frequently relocate. Although he was too old to serve the army, he was still sentenced to spend seven years behind bars due to draft evasion.

. . .

The Rise of Elijah Muhammad

Elijah Muhammad reclaimed his position with the Nation of Islam in the 1940s. With his new position now requiring more time, Malcolm began training intensively and quit his day job. Before quitting the Ford Motor Company, Malcolm had fully developed his orator skills, which prompted Elijah to entrust him with founding the Nation's temple in Boston. After moving to Boston, Malcolm proceeded in his efforts to convert as many of his friends and family members as he could. While he did manage to reconnect with his sister Ella and his friend Shorty, they didn't convert.

After establishing the Nation's temple in Boston, Elijah then sent Malcolm to Philadelphia to proceed with doing the organization's work. Malcolm came to New York in 1954, to find out that his old friends, Sammy the Pimp and Archie suffered a difficult fate. While Sammy died, Archie was dying, and his initial efforts to spread teachings across New York faced obstacles. Initially, people didn't respond well to his teachings, but Malcolm wouldn't give up. He realized that this particular population needed a different approach, so he and his peers adopted different techniques. Upon changing their approach, they had more success in advocating the idea of African Americans returning to Africa, to their roots. Malcolm realized that Christians responded better to a more refined way of speaking, so he changed his orator style and began emphasizing how Christianity contributed to the oppression of African Americans.

The Nation of Islam gained public recognition after an incident in which one of its members was attacked. After a police attack on one of their members, the organization's youth group called "Fruit of Islam" held a mass demonstration outside the precinct where their companion was being held. They proceeded to protest outside the hospital in which the victim was treated and went on to win a $70.000 lawsuit against the city of New York. At this time, Malcolm had taken a vow of poverty and was using only the necessary resources to supply for his family's basic living needs. His humble approach to life earned him access to the organization's resources, but he didn't own any of his own. Instead, he focused on raising the temples across the country and managed to raise temples in New York, Detroit, and Chicago by 1965.

THE BRAVE NEW MAN

The few 'luxuries' that Malcolm possessed included his eyeglasses, a suitcase, and a wristwatch. He purchased these items after leaving the Massachusetts prison. They symbolized his newfound sense of discipline and devotion to time and efficiency. They were also a sign that his vision had evolved and matured and signaled his devotion and drive to do his work. His prison conversion was noticeable through peaceful surrender to police forces, and obtaining his few possessions symbolized the beginning of his political career and the growth of his authority.

Despite being poorly educated before going to prison, Malcolm talked about a feeling of intuition about the upcoming change, which prompted him to accept his sentence peacefully. The few items he collected after leaving prison were characteristic for people in his trade, and getting them marked his devotion to doing the work he was about to devote his life to. They also marked a transformation toward a more self-aware and responsible Malcolm, who was thinking not only about the Nation of Islam and its teachings but also contemplated broader issues.

These three items, his eyeglasses, wristwatch, and suitcase, were broadly discussed among those who analyzed Malcolm's work in later years. They were also observed as a sign that his career has begun. However, each of the objects had its own, individual meaning.

Malcolm's wristwatch was an invaluable part of his daily routine, and he depended on it to complete his busy schedule. He was devoted to showing commitment to everyone he met, and a part of showing that commitment was being punctual. However, unlike his predecessors, he didn't distance himself from people he knew before his transformation. He took time out of his day to reconnect with his family and maintained a harmonious familial circle throughout his life.

Malcolm rarely parted from his suitcase, which signified that his life consisted of constant movement and growth, but also that all of his time was devoted to doing the work for the organization. His main work consisted of traveling across the country and preaching to his fellow African Americans in effort to convert them.

When it comes to the symbolism of Malcolm's eyeglasses, they are a representation of the clarity that he was searching for in life. Aside from that, they are often understood as a symbol of him correcting his view of the world, and political and racial issues. This shift in his mindset shaped his devotion to understanding the connections between people and shaping his insights into messages that would appeal to the masses. Overall, his modest, uniform, and effective appearance served to help him focus on what he perceived to be his cause, and mentally distanced himself from the behaviors he once displayed and the person he no longer wanted to be. Overall, his appearance represented the new path he was about to take in life. This was influenced, or at least was mirrored in Elijah Muhammad comparing him to Biblical Job, who suffered numerous trials but still had resisted temptations. Malcolm later reflected on this parallel and expressed how his different life experiences tested his faith, and how he overcame numerous obstacles with faith in God. He often used this story to point out that a transformation is possible and that betterment is possible for anyone willing to make a change. In many ways, Malcolm actually followed a similar path to his father. He witnessed his father's devotion as a child, and although his childhood was plagued by tragedy, it was the loss of his father that had truly devastated it, resulting in a series of events that eventually landed him in prison.

The Unshakeable Faith

Malcolm had Elijah Muhammad as his role model and mentor, whose encouragement and recognition shaped and improved Malcolm's own perception of himself. Although Malcolm's studies and improvements were, indeed, a result of his independent effort, one must wonder if having a surrogate-father present in his life, first Bimbi and later Elijah Muhammad, was the paternal influence that he needed in order to recognize and choose to live a modest, orderly, non-violent life. Malcolm's success in working with the Nation was also his own making, but it was made possible by his mentor, and the validation that he got from Elijah was likely to have given him wings to proceed to find purpose in living a modest life.

Malcolm's admiration of Elijah continued to grow throughout the years, and his later recollections state he saw Elijah as more than a human. He observed Elijah Muhammad as a deity, whose acceptance and approval was a reward that helped keep Malcolm out of legal trouble and increased his desire to respond with an equal amount of appreciation as was given to him. Malcolm was struck by Elijah's confidence and felt divine-like devotion toward him, believing in him even more than Elijah believed in himself. This unshakable faith and idolization of Elijah will later prove to be the downfall of a long friendship, when Elijah proves not to be the ideal figure that Malcolm suspected him to be. Being disappointed in Elijah will later cause Malcolm to question his beliefs, and eventually distance himself from the Nation of Islam.

In 1957, Malcolm founded the Nation's newspaper, "Muhammad Speaks". The paper attracted a lot of publicity in 1959 after the book titled *The Black Muslims in America* was published by C. Eric Lincoln. Simultaneously, a television show on the Nation presented the organization in an extreme light. This enraged Malcolm and was a learning experience about the type of misinformation that can be spread by the media. More newspapers began writing about the Nation, keeping Malcolm busy with having to answer phone calls and defend the organization from bias. He focused on clarifying the issues and making counterchages. His workload increased since he was starting to get more frequently invited to participate in lectures and on panels by different organizations.

In 1959, Malcolm began traveling the globe. He spread his mission outside the US and traveled to Ghana, Nigeria, Sudan, Arabia, and Egypt. Expanding their views outside the US exposed Malcolm to more radical beliefs, and it also affected Elijah's perception of other leaders. Malcolm's increased intolerance toward integration-oriented leaders was further infused by the growing attacks on the Nation of Islam, which eventually drove Elijah to abandon his more tolerant beliefs regarding integration advocates. Elijah eventually allowed Malcolm to express his opinions openly, which grew in frustration and radicalism. This led to massive rallies being held by 1960. These rallies initially admitted only Black people, but then began admitting White news reporters, and eventually anyone who was willing to join.

The more the Nation grew in militance and size, the more attention it brought upon itself. The police and FBI began investigating the organization and its participants. They used numerous techniques to obtain information about their activities, including infiltration and telephone tapping. Malcolm's phone was also tapped, and he became a person of interest for the authorities. A large part of the government's interest in monitoring the Nation came from the fact that many of its members were former or current prisoners. The success behind the Nation's ability to recruit prisoners can be attributed to numerous factors. Being in prison conditioned Black inmates to reflect on their position in society and how the White people at the time affected their lives. Second, the prison environment dictated discipline and kept inmates from living disorganized lives. This would motivate them to change to a more adaptive, organized lifestyle that aligned with the Nation's principles. Despite extremely negative views on the society they were living in, Nation members adopted quite strict, modest, and conservative life principles, which helped reform many inmates, and even helped plenty of them recover from drug addiction.

The Fall From Grace

Elijah Muhammad's declining health prompted the Nation to purchase him a house in Arizona, where he could spend the majority of the year. His distance and illness, now combined with the increasing workload of the Nation, put Malcolm into the powerful position of making the majority of important decisions. The organization gained more and more publicity by 1963, and Malcolm became one of the most in-demand university lecturers. He enjoyed these engagements and was excited about intellectual confrontations at universities.

However, this drove a wedge between him and Elijah Muhammed, who didn't approve of him participating in lecture circuits. Simultaneously, other members of the Nation accused Malcolm of trying to take over the organization, and he was less and less featured in the newspaper of his own making, Muhammad Speaks. Malcolm made efforts to reduce the tension between him and Elijah by reducing his public appearances, but his relationship with the organization proceeded to complicate. The issue was made worse when Elijah Muhammad faced paternity suits. Allegedly, he fathered children with two of the temple's secretaries, which he denied. Malcolm attempted to ignore the allegations, thinking that they were merely efforts to undermine Elijah. When he eventually confronted Elijah about the allegations, he implicitly confessed but hadn't publicly taken accountability for his actions. With Elijah's refusal to reveal the truth to his organization, Malcolm's faith in Elijah was shaken even further.

CHAPTER 5: THE HAJJ TRAVEL AND SPIRITUAL TRANSFORMATION

Malcolm found out that every Muslim should go on a pilgrimage at least once in their life, to make his own journey to *hajj* in Mecca, Saudi Arabia. However, to get a hajj visa, Malcolm first needed to have his Muslim status approved by the Muslim United Nations advisor, Mahmoud Youssef Shawarbi. First, Malcolm went to Cairo for sightseeing. When he flew to

Saudi Arabia, officials in Jedda confiscated his passport and told him that his status as a true Muslim would first need to be established by a high court.

While waiting for the situation to resolve, Malcolm was sent to an airport dormitory, where he reflected on the multitude of languages, customs, and colors he noticed on the people around him. Once his situation was resolved, Malcolm was pleasantly surprised by the hospitality of Omar Azzam, who he turned to for help. Azzam gave Malcolm a suite at the Jedda Palace hotel that belonged to his father. Malcolm was fascinated by the hospitality and enjoyed conversations with the elite. He was lent a car by Prince Faisal, a prince of Saudi Arabia. His visit instilled a sense of wonder, particularly at the lack of racial division in Mecca. Malcolm hasn't experienced a non-segregated life before, nor had he witnessed two races coexisting without tensions. This changed his perspective on racial issues.

When Malcolm returned to the US, he had built a perspective that there are White people who haven't been afflicted by racism. This helped him realize that racial problems in the US were generated as a result of the long history of racism and racial violence in America. Inspired by his experience in Mecca, Malcolm first started signing as El-Hajj Malik El-Shabazz, which he later adopted as his official name. Still, the public continued to refer to him as Malcolm X. He now believed that Islam was the right solution to all problems in America.

. . .

BROADENED HORIZONS

The journey to hajj led Malcolm to realize that African Americans in the US had been robbed of the awareness that there are prosperous Black people and cultures all around the world and stripped of the identity that was innate to them. He also learned that non-White leaders and intellectuals were interested in issues surrounding African Americans. He then traveled to Ghana and Lebanon, where he was given ceremonial robes and was warmly received by the city's high commissioner. After this, Malcolm visited Morocco, Liberia, and Senegal (DeCaro, 1996). However, upon returning to the US, he faced further obstacles. During his time away, riots broke out in the US and the press blamed Malcolm, believing that he had instigated the civil unrest.

In Islam, pilgrimage plays a central role. It is more important than in the Christian and post-biblical Judaic traditions. Hajj is one of the five pillars of Islam and is considered to be a life-altering experience. Although recommended, hajj isn't compulsory as the remaining four pillars as it requires substantial financing. If a Muslim has problems with financing the hajj, they are excused from undertaking a pilgrimage. The hajj serves a purpose to symbolically, and literally, separate a pilgrim from their ordinary life and take them on a spiritual journey. The more important role that the hajj plays concerns learning about Islam and expanding already existing knowledge. A pilgrim will get to know numerous Islamic traditions that they haven't been able to experience or learn in the past. Muslim pilgrims are known to return dramatically changed from their hajj experience, which is even more emphasized in the modern day than it was in the more conservative era when Malcolm lived.

For Malcolm, hajj was a life-altering experience. He was introduced to Islam while in prison, and his perception of the world, life, and religion was shaped by his strong Baptist father. He spent the majority of his adult life in urban surroundings, and, in spiritual terms, he experienced a great fall into moral depravity after being separated from his mother. To understand how the hajj journey contrasted everything that Malcolm had seen, heard of, and experienced before, it is also important to note that Malcolm also briefly believed in militant doctrines and practices. Although the Nation's movement grew to be very powerful and was based on Islam, it grew in 1930's Detroit. As such, its interpretations of Islam deviated from true Islam, particularly given that the organization's founder Wallace Fard was of mysterious origins and linked with the Moorish Science Temple. This Temple had Masonic traits in its rhetoric and imagery, suggesting that the connection to authentic Shiite or Sunni Islam was distant and loose. Malcolm witnessed this as well, which could have been the first of many contributing elements to his altering and eventually decaying relationship with the Nation. While the Nation was based on the Islamic principles, it heavily emphasized discipline, and the other elements of Islam weren't as emphasized as they would have been in other Muslim environments.

In particular, the Nation's interpretation of Islam was purposefully geared toward African Americans, whereas Islam as a religion was open to all races and ethnicities. Also, the Nation's proclaimed values and rhetoric revolved around battling racism, whereas Islam as a religion proclaimed an entire context of interpreting life, reality, and one's own place and role in it on an internal, individual level.

Leaving the Nation of Islam

Malcolm decided to go on a pilgrimage after suffering a personal, spiritual crisis. This crisis came after Malcolm was silenced by Elijah Muhammad for giving a controversial statement regarding the murder of President Kennedy. This event was the beginning of the end of Malcolm's relationship with Elijah and the Nation, which shook some of his core beliefs. Malcolm's faith was heavily tested in the weeks that followed the President's murder. The Nation's rhetoric was otherwise strong, honest, and they didn't refrain from speaking difficult truths whenever it was necessary. But, after President Kennedy's murder, Elijah Muhammad wanted to maintain a peaceful, respectful atmosphere. He considered the President to be the leader of the Nation's members, who were a part of the country, and thought that any fiery commentary would be disrespectful.

Conversion to Sunni Islam

Some evidence suggests that Elijah was aware of the FBI's interest in the organization, and didn't want to do anything that would further deepen the suspicions towards him and his followers. Malcolm, on the other hand, found this attitude to be hypocritical and against the interest of Black Americans. He thought that refraining from speaking his truth would be dishonorable, and not in the Nation's spirit. But, there is another reason why Malcolm's statement angered Elijah so much as to practically banish him from the Nation.

His statement was disobedient, and disobedience was not to be tolerated. In this sense, Malcolm found himself heavily burdened and torn between honoring his mentoring and staying true to himself. He chose to stay true to himself, for which he was accused of aspiring to step on the person who helped him climb higher than would have been possible hadn't it been for Elijah. Faced with an impossible choice, Malcolm officially broke from the Nation in 1964 and founded his own Muslim Mosque. At the same time, he founded the Organization of Afro-American Unity, which was a secular organization. This further distanced him from the Nation as the organization that admitted non-Muslim African Americans. After this, he converted to Sunni Islam.

Before planning to make the hajj in 1964, Malcolm wasn't familiar with many basic Islamic traditions. For example, he was unaware of *salat*, the five-time daily praying custom. In Egypt, he met with Mahmoud Youssef Shawarbi, who was a scholar. Under Mahmoud Youssef's mentorship, Malcolm further distanced himself from the Nation's doctrine. Only after Malcolm's knowledge of Islam had been corrected was a hajj visa been granted to him. While Malcolm faced some difficulties on his arrival in Jeddah, Malcolm's studies with Dr. Shawarbi earned him an admittance with Prince Faisal, and the company of a *mutawwif*, a hajj guide who showed new pilgrims how to perform numerous rites.

Malcolm was first struck by the diversity of Muslims in Mecca's Sacred Mosque. He observed the Muslims of various genders, races, ethnicities, and cultures. There, he became aware that the term 'Muslim' encompassed a plurality of ethnicities and races. This deepened the knowledge he was given by Dr. Shawarbi and helped him develop his understanding of what it meant to be a Muslim. The hajj is considered to be a pivotal time in Malcolm's life. It was the time he learned true Islam and began advocating for a plural, diverse, and tolerant overview of the world.

Sadly, it was the practice of Sunni Islam and the resulting change in Malcolm's rhetoric that angered Elijah Muhammad the most. Further chapters of this book will ponder upon different factors that played a role in Malcolm's murder. But, it is considered that his distancing from the Nation's doctrine and Elijah's open criticism of Malcolm planted the seed for his eventual murder. Although no proof that Elijah Muhammad was in any way an instigator of his murder, scholars and followers alike claim that given Elijah's strong influence and adoration by followers, his discontent with Malcolm would have been sufficient to drive someone to murder. Those who still recall their time with the Nation remember feeling like Malcolm betrayed Elijah and disrespected not only his personality but also everything that Elijah had done for the members of the Nation. Although the Nation's doctrine differed from true Islam, it helped many straighten out their lives, recover from addiction, and begin living 'clean', structured, productive lives. Hundreds of thousands of African Americans saw Elijah as a savior and were profoundly hurt by Malcolm's criticism of him and his teachings. This frustration would eventually grow to cause death threats, and finally, make those threats reality.

Overall, Malcolm's hajj resulted in three key changes in his life:

Insight Into True Islam

Before being taught true Islam, Malcolm's view of the religion came from a view on Islam that was radicalized greatly compared to the source religion. While the discipline it would foster had initial benefits for hundreds of thousands of African Americans, it kept them from reaching their true heights and blocked spiritual development. Islam, similar to Christianity and Judaism, when taught correctly, secures abundant spiritual growth, and records of health, financial, social, and spiritual benefits for true believers are even recorded in science. Elijah Muhammad's perception of Islam leaned more to how the individual serves the community, or his organization, whereas true Islam helps a Muslim live a healthy, happy, peaceful, and wholesome life. Malcolm learned this during his hajj travel, and the knowledge he passed on earned him an immense following upon his return.

Change in Philosophy

Malcolm's outlook on life practically flipped upside-down. He began seeing problems of race, segregation, and discrimination as universally present across the world. He began to view them from a more social perspective, understanding that there were parts of the world where other non-White people suffered the same fate regardless of difficult circumstances. Such insight was helpful for African Americans to truly understand how to combat discrimination. The answer in overcoming racism, as Malcolm learned, was knowledge and education, and not religion or battle.

Break-Away From Elijah and the Nation

Altogether, the transformation that Malcolm underwent didn't sit well with Elijah Muhammad. It not only undermined his authority, but he was also afraid that he would lose followers. Considering how influential the Nation had grown, and the number of businesses and wealth it had in its control, such events could, in Elijah's mind, undercut everything that so many of his followers worked so hard to build. Malcolm's plural, international outlook on the world jeopardized a closed bubble that Elijah helped his followers create. This narrow focus on living, socializing, and financially supporting the Nation's followers helped their entrepreneur business owners accumulate a lot of income. If his followers believed Malcolm when he said that they should open to new experiences and cultures, this self-sustaining ecosystem would have been compromised.

Malcolm died less than a year after his hajj pilgrimage. When he returned to the US, the attacks on him became more serious and more severe than ever. However, the little time he had to spread the word about his new insights had set the fight for racial equality and justice on a new trajectory.

CHAPTER 6: STRUGGLE FOR CIVIL RIGHTS

Malcolm's ultimate departure from the Nation of Islam happened after his controversial statement regarding the assassination of John F. Kennedy. Elijah Muhammad ordered his ministers not to comment on the assassination, but Malcolm made a controversial statement about the murder being the example of "chickens coming home to roost." This enraged Elijah, who silenced Malcolm for 90 days as a punishment for disobeying his order (DeCaro, 1996). However, Malcolm began to suspect that the organization was plotting to cast him off and even heard rumors about them planning to assassinate him. These suspicions were proven accurate. One of Malcolm's assistants admitted to being ordered to kill him and ultimately decided to distance himself from the organization. Malcolm later concluded that Elijah's outrage concerning his statement on the Kennedy murder was merely a smokescreen to hide the plot against him. He realized that he had been betrayed by Elijah and decided to distance himself from the Nation.

Soul Searching

After separating from the Nation, Malcolm looked for some peace and clarity. He decided to accept an invitation from Cassius Clay, a boxer, who invited him and his family to stay with him in Florida while he prepared for one of his fights. The time the two of them spent together strengthened both of their faiths. Clay was struck by Malcolm's training skills, willpower, and sharp might. He converted to Islam and changed his name to Muhammad Ali after his fight.

The more Malcolm spent time with Muhammad Ali, the more he became estranged from the Nation of Islam. He began focusing on the economic and political interests of African Americans.

African American Unity

Malcolm's views evolved to search for universal justice, regardless of criteria such as class or race. He began holding meetings in Harlem, within his new organization, The Organization for Afro-American Unity. This organization was inclusive of religions but admitted only Black people. Malcolm believed that African Americans should first unite within their own organizations before joining White people to face racism. After this, Malcolm spent nearly five months in the Middle East again, where he met numerous world leaders. This is when he began to feel burdened by his reputation and started to suspect that death was near. Although he was writing an autobiography, he expressed his doubts that he would ever finish it.

Malcolm's worldly experiences helped transform his views on race and equality. Unlike before, he now believed that African Americans should view themselves as one among many minorities who were looking for justice. After visiting multiple countries in Africa that won independence from colonial forces, Malcolm expanded his vision of the civil rights movement in the context of Islam. Malcolm realized that the religious principles he learned in Africa and the Middle East can be applied to the US. He became determined to bring charges in front of the UN tribunal against the US for mass violations of human rights.

Minority Civil Rights

Further development of his views began to include racial and ethnic bias against other minority groups, not just African Americans. Malcolm begins to see that other forms of discrimination and bias were present against the Dutch, Jewish, Italian, and German people. However, he felt like the adversity toward African Americans was more difficult to overcome, and the prejudice was rooted more deeply than with the other groups. However, Malcolm still believed that Africans living in other parts of the world faced more difficult struggles than other minority groups since ethnic minorities hadn't experienced that severe level of enslavement, discrimination, and oppression.

Toward the end of his life, Malcolm began understanding how the change he made in prison was similar to how his later views evolved. In prison, he abandoned his street ways and embraced religion, knowledge, and education. Later in life, he abandoned radicalism and broadened his views on civil rights and equality for African Americans and other minorities alike. Once he was released from jail, Malcolm had the vision to unify African Americas as people in their fight for economic and political improvement. However, visiting the Middle East offered new views and a glimpse of life without racial segregation and tension. After witnessing a life without racial segregation, he began to believe that Islam offered a color-blind future which led him to accept the idea of racial integration. He changed his attitude toward integration and became convinced that overcoming oppression would require non-White nations and groups to unite.

Despite coming from an underprivileged background, Malcolm possessed the intelligence and wisdom to change his beliefs whenever he experienced a different truth. This helped him grow and mature as an individual and as a visionary and orator. His willingness to change proved that he was far more than an angry revolutionary. He was after vengeance while it was the only way to get the justice that was known to him. As Malcolm began learning other ways of life and other forms of achieving justice, vengeance became irrelevant. He now began looking for ways to help people live in racial harmony.

Malcolm was the Nation's fiercest advocate for Black Nationalism for the majority of his career. He often challenged Martin Luther King's non-violent, multiracial approach. Although he never called for violence directly, it was considered that his tone and rhetoric sparked tactical and ideological conflicts within the Black freedom activists of the 1960s. Malcolm X and Martin Luther King had drastically different views on solving racial problems, with King advocating for integration and Malcolm believing in racial separatism. Still, there was respect between the two men. Despite all of the differences in views and philosophies, Malcolm's views on race and racial problems grew and evolved. While he never fully agreed with King regarding how to solve the problems of Black Americans, he eventually accepted the idea that plurality, although maybe not in the terms as King's philosophy, was a better solution for Black Americans than separatism. While Malcolm X may have not agreed with the King's philosophy, he respected him as a leader of Black Americans. He would even send King articles written by the Nation of Islam and would invite him to attend early 1960's mass meetings. It bothered Malcolm that King advocated the philosophy of "loving your enemy", and he didn't believe much in the effectiveness of this strategy. Martin Luther King sought to bridge the gap between races by understanding but seeing the real-life struggles and violence that his fellow Black Americans endured, Malcolm didn't believe in this. He believed that King's views stemmed from his privileged background and that a different lifeline and upbringing skewed King's view on the severity of the situation.

Malcolm's intellectual curiosity and desire to test his beliefs is certainly admirable. Since he and NOI had completely different views from M.L.K., Malcolm wanted to have discussions, and would frequently invite King to attend Elijah's speeches. He wanted Black people in America to have an open platform and hear discussions about their problems. Although King never responded to his letters and invitations, King also respected Malcolm. After Malcolm's death, King wrote to Betty Shabazz. King expressed his sadness over Malcolm's death, saying that he had a deep affection for her late husband. King also respected Malcolm's ability to observe, analyze, and understand the cause of the problems he witnessed.

If we were to learn anything from Malcolm, it was his intellectual curiosity. He didn't seek to be right at all costs. He didn't gain a following by telling people what they wanted to hear, nor did he rely on battling his opponents in order to gain a reputation. His fight was symbolic and intellectual, and his respect for anyone he encountered was immense. He initiated a dialogue with people who didn't agree with him, and he was interested in discussions and public debates. Today's public discourse, sadly, is driven by a desire to win at all cost and manipulating the facts to make a point is common for many civil rights leaders and activists. Malcolm was a person of integrity, and he wouldn't diminish his own self-esteem by using manipulation. Instead, he believed that his fellow Black Americans deserved to have multiple leaders and hear multiple viewpoints on each of their problems. This might have been a more difficult route to follow, but it established him as a respectable individual.

After Malcolm's separation from the Nation of Islam in 1964 and his pilgrimage to Mecca, Malcolm combined political action with his leadership skills to advocate for civil rights. Martin Luther King commented that the fallout between the two leaders didn't affect the civil rights movement and that he believed that certain African Americans might resort to more radical actions if there was a lack of real, tangible progress regarding Black civil rights visible to each and every member of the community.

A short while after making this statement, Martin Luther King met with Malcolm X during the Senate's 1964 Civil Rights Act debate. The two men shook hands, and King later stated that he held a position of reconciliation and kindness with an adversary. While there was now a little less tension between the two leaders, and Malcolm's views had changed significantly, he still sought to establish connections with more militant-oriented Black leaders. He then began meeting the Student Nonviolent Coordinating Committee works, which included Fannie Lou Hamer, their Mississippi organizer, and John Lewis, the chairman of the organization.

He was still inspired after and sought to revive the Black Nationalist movement. In an interview in 1965, Malcolm expressed his support for any group that worked toward achieving immediate, meaningful results. He was interested in making real, immediate actions toward solving the problems or racial equality. After Martin Luther King was arrested in Alabama, Malcolm traveled there to meet Coretta Scott King to show the unity and strength of the Black civil rights movement. He believed that his presence and the prospect of a militant response to King's peaceful efforts would make the authorities more willing to hear King out. Malcolm died only a couple of weeks after these events, and King expressed great regret that the assassination occurred right after Malcolm began understanding the nonviolent movement. Malcolm's death sparked further battles between his and King's followers over their opposing ideologies.

. . .

Plurality of Ideologies

In order to understand Malcolm's views on Black civil rights, it's important to note that several leaders had quite opposing views on the situation. Malcolm led Black Muslims, while King appealed to southern Christian African Americans. Much of Malcolm's followers didn't identify with the philosophy of Martin Luther King. In general, both Malcom X and King had the same civil rights goals. They wanted to empower African Americans and defeat racism. However, they had different speaking venues, with Malcolm giving speeches at street corners and King doing so in churches, and they also had different visions. Malcolm didn't see himself as an American and wanted to separate society for his followers. He didn't want to integrate into White America and didn't believe that any progress could be made using a non-violent approach. To him, being non-violent meant being defenseless, and he didn't believe that African Americans should ever stop practicing self-defense against the police.

Criticism of Martin Luther King

Malcolm believed that King's teachings lead African Americans to be defenseless in the face of the White police violence. He also believed that Christianity was a religion of White people and that it was taught to African Americans as a way of keeping them tame and subdued. On the other hand, leaders of non-violent civil rights movements often saw the militant side as thugs, believing that the Nation of Islam was being paid by Arab groups to gather criminals around an ideology. Martin Luther King rarely commented on Malcolm, as he wished to keep his public speeches within the positive action scope, avoiding engaging in consistent negative debate.

Responding to 'Hypocrisy'

Malcolm became less critical of M.L.K. over time and grew closer with the civil rights movement as he was becoming more distant from Elijah Muhammad. After the shooting of Ronald Stokes, a Los Angeles Temple secretary by the police, Elijah Muhammad wouldn't allow any aggressive response. Malcolm felt provoked by this lack of response, expressing that action was necessary in order to avenge the crime. Here, Malcolm began to talk about how the Nation of Islam engaged in fierce rhetoric but rarely took any actions when needed. Around this time, he also began accusing Elijah Muhammad's children of living a luscious life from the Nation's funds, suggesting that there was an ulterior motive to their words and actions.

CHAPTER 7: MARTIN LUTHER KING

Malcolm X lived a quite different life compared to Martin Luther King Jr. The two never saw eye to eye when it came to philosophy and politics, and they only met once.

. . .

How Malcolm X Met Martin Luther King Jr.

The fact that Martin Luther King Jr and Malcolm X worked to fulfill the same goal and belonged to the same movement yet were still unable to work together is strange by today's standards, to say the least. However, during the 50s and 60s, Malcolm X and Martin Luther King met for one time only, and even that bordered on accidental. After Washington's Senate civil rights debate was over on March 26, 1964, Malcolm slipped out to meet King as he was walking out of a conference room. The two greeted each other politely, and then the press started swarming around them to take pictures. It is said that King looked surprised, and Malcolm's confident grin was followed by a silent commentary that King was now going to be investigated as a result of the meeting. After the encounter, the two parted ways and never met each other again (Carson, 2005).

But, the tensions between them weren't only rooted in their philosophies. Malcolm and King came from different backgrounds and had different upbringings and life experiences. The different lifestyles the two men led established a difference in their views long before they joined the civil rights movement. Matin was four years younger than Malcolm. Similar to Malcolm, his father was a Baptist preacher who spoke against racism. Martin was taught resistance toward the current position of Black Americans since the earliest years of his life, much like Malcolm. Although both men suffered obstacles and discrimination, Martin's life wasn't nearly as traumatic as Malcolm's. Unlike in Malcolm's family, Martin grew up feeling loved and supported within his familial circle, which he stated had instilled in him a sense of optimism regarding life and human nature.

Martin's life growing up was a stark contrast to that of Malcolm's. While Malcolm's father was murdered in 1931 by White supremacists, and his mother was eventually committed into an asylum after suffering a mental breakdown, leaving him to grow up with foster parents, Martin's family was prosperous throughout the Great Depression. While Martin also suffered as a result of racism, which he recalled almost drove him to suicide, he had a loving family to turn to. He also recalled his father was able to help him if he got into any trouble. He also admits to never lacking anything in life and never feeling out of place.

Malcolm went to Michigan White schools, where he studied alongside mostly White children and teachers. He didn't have a chance to study within his Black community, which caused him to develop an inferiority complex. Malcolm recalled feeling miserable and out of place almost all the time while he was attending school. Martin, on the other hand, attended mostly Black schools. He grew up feeling a proud African American, and he was in an environment where he could see and experience his own success, and also model after Black teachers and role models. He was encouraged to succeed, whereas Malcolm was once told by one of his White teachers that he didn't stand a chance at becoming a lawyer because he was Black. As a result of this, Martin likely grew up feeling connected to his community. He had a sense of pride for who he was, but he also felt like he could fit into the White surroundings as Black and an equal.

As a young adult, Malcolm got involved with crime and was later imprisoned. Since he didn't finish school, there was not much opportunity for him, and he also didn't have parental guidance and support. He only changed his ways once he found guidance and support from people who believed in him. Martin's young adulthood was a contrast to Malcolm's as well. He went to university and found much more inspiring role models in his civil rights struggle, which shaped his philosophy in a different direction. Being a Baptist leader, Martin also had a greater chance of success, given that the majority of African Americans at the time were Baptist. Martin was a leader to a much larger following, while Malcolm, although he did find acceptance and support with the Nation of Islam, still belonged to a much smaller group.

Martin and Malcolm first learned about each other during the 1950s and started publicly disagreeing in 1957. The Nation's representatives wanted to meet with the representatives of the Southern Christian Leadership Conference under Martin's leadership but were rejected. Although Malcolm tried to get in contact with

Martin—even inviting him to debate—Martin continuously ignored them which frustrated Malcolm. He believed that, despite obvious differences in opinions, the two sides should work together to provide solid leadership for African Americans. He wanted to work around their differences in opinion, and even assured Martin that the debate would be organized to secure orderly and polite communication. He also stated that he believed in the unity of Black people regardless of religious differences and that Martin shouldn't allow himself to be persuaded against Muslim Blacks by White people.

At the time, the press took Martin's side, and saw him as the "good guy", labeling Malcolm as a Black supremacist. The media sensationalism played a role in deepening the wedge between the two leaders. Martin was strongly against the radical approach present within the Nation, and he even wrote to his followers from prison to warn them against either staying passive or going to the extreme of Black nationalism. He preached for non-violent protesting and love as the best way forward for African Americans.

Around this time, Malcolm started to get frustrated with NOI's isolationism, and he saw it as against the interests of African Americans. He disagreed with the Nation disallowing their members to participate in the civil rights movement, and he also disagreed with members being unable to join civil rights protests and political events. Malcolm began to think that the organization he was a part of was strong in word but not in deed. He believed that this wasn't the way to get change. Malcolm wanted to get Martin's attention, and he tried to do that by criticizing his methods. Martin eventually replied as he could no longer ignore his opponent's attacks. He responded by expressing understanding for the traumatic experiences Malcolm had, stating that he was a product of violence and hate, which resulted from an oppressed life, injustice, and poverty. He acknowledged that Malcolm's frustration represented a large portion of African Americans and that the same struggles plagued many young Africans. However, Martin noticed that Malcolm had drive and intelligence that needed channeling, describing Malcolm as articulate and bright. Still, he didn't believe in the revolution that Malcolm was preaching, as he believed that violence was never the answer. Martin also stated that he would want to hear Malcolm speak on other issues than violence since he didn't believe that violence could solve the problems of African Americans.

In 1963, Malcolm was suspended from his service in the Nation of Islam and went on his pilgrimage in 1964. He was no longer the Nation's member, and he had given up on his Black supremacist views. He became a true Muslim and became more open to working together with Martin. Martin commented that he was pleased to see that a talented man such as Malcolm was abandoning racism. After this, Malcolm formed his own organization that advocated for civil rights and made sure that it was more inclusive of different people of color. He was particularly interested in those who were members of the movement. His sudden meeting with Martin Luther King was a result of his efforts. The two men only began to reconcile and express friendly opinions for one another, when Malcolm was unexpectedly assassinated. This hurt Martin deeply, and he didn't spare words showing how much he regretted Malcolm's death. However, both the press and their followers remained unaware of the animosity between the two leaders at the time.

As a result of the two different philosophies that were offered, future generations were offered the choice between the two different paths. One was the path of peace, love, and tolerance preached by Martin Luther King Jr., and the other was the direction of proactive protest and radicalism that Malcolm was best known for. The public was unaware of how much Malcolm had been interested in getting in touch with Martin, and the nature of their relationship cast a shadow on the fact that, according to many scholars, Malcolm's extremism actually helped Martin succeed, as he was seen as a positive contrast. Even Malcolm himself stated to Martin's wife, Coretta, that he wanted the public to see him as a worse alternative to that of Martin's teachings. History has shown that neither of the approaches was effective on its own. Both passive resistance and violence had a role to play in the fight for civil rights, and they still do.

The tumultuous relationship between the two leaders may have been short-lived, but their daughters carried it on in order to honor their fathers' visions. Attallah Shabazz and Yolanda King got together in 1983 to form a theater group that presented the work of their fathers in community centers, churches, and schools across the US. The two women also reflected on the fact that, despite the leaders' supposed animosity, both of them showed support for each other's families in the time of need. Malcolm contacted King's wife when he was arrested, and Martin wrote to Betty Shabazz to express his sadness after Malcolm was killed. The women agreed that African Americans would have seen a much brighter future had their fathers had an opportunity to work together for a longer period of time.

Today, we know that structural racism still exists in the US. Much has changed since the 1960s, but African Americans are still left on the fringes of society, and are continuously subject to blatant or covert racism. Today, we don't see King's and Malcolm's views as polar opposites. We see them as complementary, understanding that neither of the directions would've been sufficient on its own. We understand that long-term growth and progress require working toward peace, tolerance, and understanding, but we also acknowledge that courage is necessary when justice fails. It's been over a century since Malcolm's murder, and Black

Americans still face discrimination and police violence. It appears that different aspects of racism persist despite legal and academic efforts to explain the simple fact that all people are equally worthy.

The debate that lives on long after its creators have passed away is whether the right way to battle racism is to resist or react. People may not agree on the effectiveness of each particular method, but what can be said for both of the leaders is that they came from a place of a good intention and honesty. At the beginning of this chapter, we talked about the differences between Martin and Malcolm. Long after their passing, it is the similarities that live on.

One important thing that we can learn from them is that there's no need to go to extremes in one direction or another. There's no reason to choose to be only reactive and violent or to strip yourself of defense in order to embrace extreme specificity. Both of these can be useful tools to wield as necessary. Resistance won wars, tore down entire regimes, and helped seek justice when officials were uninterested in doing so. On the other hand, at the time of peace, it took knowing how to communicate, and live, and work together with everyone around to maintain the peace. Martin knew that integration is a good way to prevent conflict and avoid cruelty, and Malcolm knew that active resistance using "all means necessary" is needed to show the oppressor that abuse of power will not be tolerated. The social justice and civil rights activists of today base many of their strategies on these two different approaches.

What Can You Learn From the Relationship?

What Martin and Malcolm created left a legacy, and a clear direction for how to act in order to make an immediate change. If you want to change society, consistent work is necessary to point out injustices, and pacifist methods are the best way to break prejudice and unveil misconceptions. Pacifist methods of spreading awareness, advocating, and teaching, are what help build a just perspective on any topic. However, there will always be resistance to change by those who don't wish a group to assume its rights.

What we know today is that people can only change their views and ways willingly. The truth is, no matter how much we know today, many people will still choose to remain racist. They will still choose to live within their own circles and might be against diversity. The reason for this is that people form beliefs, not only based on what they were taught and what they experienced, but also based on what makes them feel good. It's not so difficult to understand that people want to keep those beliefs that make them feel just and superior. For some, it's not White supremacy, and it is not Black supremacy that keeps others from facing the demons that plague each human, regardless of their race and ethnicity: fear and low self-esteem.

Today, we know that discrimination, prejudice, and racism flourish in societies that are undereducated, and for some, they are a conscious effort to advance in life or business. Having the work of leaders like Malcolm X and Martin Luther King Jr. to model after helps us understand how to look past those who remain blind to the truth, and appeal to those who are willing to question their beliefs. It helps protect us from the malicious intents of those who channel their own trauma through racism and fight for those who've been hurt when authorities choose to have each other's back instead of admitting to having rotten apples within their ranks. But, Martin's and Malcolm's teachings and rhetoric give us one more gift; they help us perceive what systematic racism is, and how it leads to criminalization and discrimination of innocent people.

CHAPTER 8: MUHAMMAD ALLI

Cassius Clay's victory over Sonny Liston marked more than just another victorious boxing match in the star's career. Clay won against all odds, and none of the spectators knew how big of a transformation for the boxer was happening behind the scene. They didn't notice a quiet, neatly dressed man in a dark suit observing the match with undivided attention. That man was Malcolm X, Clay's good friend, and mentor. That night, Cassius Clay was about to confront an opponent much bigger and stronger than him. Indeed, he trained the best he could, but a victory wasn't in sight. Still, a new mentor appeared in his life, who gave him a newfound faith. During the time Clay and Malcolm had spent together, Malcolm felt like Clay was destined to win, and he was so certain of the boxer's competence that he filled him with the strength and certainty needed to win the match.

. . .

THE BEGINNING OF THE FRIENDSHIP

Some say Malcolm approached Clay with an open heart, yet others suspect that he was also sufficiently aware of his own charisma and power of persuasion. The one who used to be mentored believed he now had a prodigy and gave all he had in empowering Clay, uplifting him, and eventually persuading him to join the Nation. Opinions remain divided regarding Malcolm's own motivation to join forces with Clay (Ezra, 2016). Cassius Clay was a rising star, but he certainly enjoyed publicity and had the potential to spread the Nation's influence. Although torn between loyalty to his estranged mentor Elijah Muhammad and his own morality, Malcolm was eager to remedy the relationship, if possible. With all his respect for Cassius Clay, Malcolm also hoped that having a figure of potential influence join the Nation's ranks would help him get closer to Elijah. He was hopeful and willing to make amends with the Nation's leader and finding a person to uplift and spread the Nation's reach seemed like a double win for Malcolm.

A day after his victory over Liston, Clay announced that he would now be called Cassius X. He had given up the last name given and inherited in slavery, taking instead the last name X to emphasize his unknown true origin. Only a month later, Cassius X announced that he had taken the name Muhammad Ali, marking his conversion to Islam.

Muhammad Ali Joins the Nation of Islam

The friendship between Muhammad Ali and Malcolm X began strong. Muhammad Ali visited the Nation's annual event, the Savior's Day rally in Chicago. The Nation's members often referred to themselves as Black Muslims, and Saxton, one of Ali's close friends, had been a member of the organization and took up a role of introducing Ali to the new scene. Malcolm held the opening speech at the rally, and his mesmerizing rhetoric appealed to Ali as well. Muhammad Ali was still young and impressionable and was stunned by the aura of authority and confidence that surrounded Malcolm X.

Malcolm, on the other hand, recognized the charisma in Cassius Clay that had the potential to draw people in, a potential that could mean more than just bringing in new members into the Nation. Serving the organization in this way, by bringing in an influential figure, could've strengthened Malcolm's reputation within his own circles, a reputation that had begun to whither after he displayed disobedience. It is important to note that the first major signs that Malcolm was being shunned by the Nation began to show. He was yet unaware of it, but Elijah's closest people, alongside his children, began calling Malcolm ambitious behind his back long before Elijah silenced him. Malcolm was losing the trust of the organization he himself helped establish, and the friendship with Muhammad Ali had the potential to remedy a lot of the damage that was done previously.

Malcolm started spending as much time as possible with Ali, and became not only his friend and brother. He was a father figure who gave Ali the type of spiritual support he felt he was lacking. Having rejected the religion of his youth, Ali now needed a mentor. However, considering how terrified the "White public" was of the Nation of Islam, Muhammad Ali kept quiet about his conversion. Before he established himself as a boxing authority, he too could have been shunned by the boxing establishment, who most likely wouldn't tolerate him being a member of the Nation. He only felt comfortable revealing his membership after beating Sonny Liston and still encountered plenty of judgment over his membership. Some of the most prominent civil rights leaders, like J. Robinson, Martin Luther King Jr., and Floyd Patterson criticized Ali over his choice. The mainstream belief was that Malcolm was setting the civil rights movement back and undermining all the great work of his predecessors.

The Fallout

The friendship between Muhammad Ali and Malcolm X was growing steadily, only to start falling apart after Malcolm's falling out with the Nation's leader, Elijah Muhammad. Ali's influence and reputation were growing strong, while at the same time, Malcolm's influence was waning. He was soon declared as undesirable by the Nation, and the turning point in the relationship between the two men was when Malcolm revealed Elijah's indiscretions to the public. After Malcolm made it public that Elijah fathered children with two of his former secretaries, he expected the public to take his side. After all, Elijah betrayed his own principles and lied to his followers. But, the devotion of the Nation's members, including Ali, was too strong to be persuaded against their mentor. Many in the Nation brushed off the scandal, turning on Malcolm instead. Malcolm was seen as a traitor who went against the one man who had given him true support and opportunities in life.

After revealing the truth about Elijah, Malcolm thought that many of the Nation's followers, including Ali, would join him and abandon Elijah. While a substantial number of former members of the Nation did follow Malcolm, Ali wasn't one of them. He turned his back on Malcolm and felt offended by Malcolm's actions. The two men never again renewed the friendship, and Malcolm felt profoundly injured and abandoned after learning how Ali felt about the situation. They only met once more after Malcolm departed from the Nation, and it was in Ghana's capital, Accra. Malcolm and Ali met outside the Ambassador Hotel, while Malcolm still wasn't aware of Ali's true feelings. Malcolm believed he was still on good terms with his friend and approached him to say hello. What he got instead of a warm greeting was a cold shoulder from Ali, who told him that he shouldn't have turned on Elijah and walked away.

Muhammad Ali regretted his words, but as he was in the company of one of Elijah Muhammad's sons, he couldn't allow himself to be seen conversing with Malcolm. Abandoning his friendship with Malcolm was one of Muhammad's greatest regrets. He regretted not making amends with Malcolm and followed a similar path after his death. Muhammad Ali too eventually abandoned the Nation and converted to Sunni Islam.

The example of Ali's and Malcolm's friendship paints an interesting picture of how politics relates to sports. According to many analysts, Ali was making a choice that was simply more convenient for him, despite feeling bonded to Malcolm. Ali's example showed that sports aren't nearly as detached from the world of politics as people would want to believe. Sport should be about people advancing strictly based on their talent, skills, and effort. Sadly, this example showed that it's not.

Some scholars indicate that Ali was making a choice that was more favorable for him. Elijah had much to offer to him in return for him joining the Nation, while Malcolm didn't have anything. Much like Muhammad Ali would bring more exposure to the Nation, the Nation would grant him support, security, and influence, none of which he could have if he sided with

Malcolm. As it turned out, Malcolm had, indeed, put all of his effort into mentoring and converting Ali, only to be rejected at the end.

Muhammad Ali went on to have a glorious career, while Malcolm died soon after their meeting in Ghana. Muhammad Ali was resentful of how their friendship ended, but it was too late for anything to change. There are a couple of important things to note from the example of how Malcolm's friendship with Muhammad Ali developed and fell.

First, Malcolm expressed great faith in Ali, his talents, and his potential. His support helped Ali through one of the most challenging fights of his career, and it also shaped his identity from there onward. But, Malcolm miscalculated two important elements in his idea that bringing Ali into the Nation would help him redeem himself.

First, Malcolm wasn't aware of the fact that Elijah's grudge with him didn't start with the Kennedy statement. It is unclear whether Elijah himself felt endangered by Malcolm's growing influence, or he was made to think this way by some other jealous members of the organization, who didn't like the fact that Malcolm was becoming more opinionated and independent. The Kennedy statement was a spark that triggered the sequence of events leading up to Malcolm's murder, but the kindling was already set months before. It became clear Malcolm's own newspaper, Muhammad Speaks, started publishing less news about him, despite him being featured heavily across the mainstream press. This began sometime before Malcolm's official silencing by Elijah. Malcolm's attempt to reconcile with Elijah in any way was doomed from the beginning, as all evidence suggests that he had long lost Elijah's trust.

Second, Malcolm saw that Muhammad Ali had much more to gain with the Nation than with him. At the time, the Nation's reputation wasn't the greatest, but Malcolm was being slammed both by the mainstream media and by the Nation. By publicly siding with Malcolm, Muhammad Ali would've put himself in the line of fire as well. Malcolm failed to understand that the friendship wasn't in the best interest of Ali's public image and sadly suffered disappointment because of that.

When thinking about what you can learn from Malcolm's example with Ali, think about reciprocity in connections and relationships. Despite his best efforts and intentions, Malcolm's ambition to befriend Ali was, indeed, an act of networking. He wanted to spread his influence through a popular sportsman, and mend his relationship with the Nation at the same time. But, the tables turned, as Malcolm miscalculated who gained from the relationship. Arguably, Ali himself regretted rejecting Malcolm, but none of that changes the fact that he couldn't make an affiliation that went against his interests. Also, the friendship was a part of a larger vision. All of Malcolm's actions aimed to unite African

Americans in a common goal, and he did manage to eventually get Ali to come on board. But, he foresaw that loyalty can sometimes overcome reason, and he couldn't predict how his brothers would react to him coming out with the truth about Elijah. He underestimated the power of persuasion. He forgot that people don't always believe even if the evidence is right under their nose, and he also couldn't guess that people would turn on him for telling the truth. He forgot the heavy price of loyalty. Elijah Muhammad was simply a stronger opponent, and relying on truth and faith, in this case, didn't help Malcolm. One could ponder upon the question of whether Malcolm's story could have ended differently had he found a better way to deal with Elijah instead of causing a scandal.

Revealing the truth at all costs isn't always the best idea, and in Malcolm's case, it proved to be fatal. One should be honest, driven, and passionate, but being patient, practical, and realistic in weighing one's options is also necessary if one is to defeat a bigger, stronger opponent. It was the strategy that ensured Ali's victory over Liston, and the lack of it that led to Malcolm losing the fight with Elijah. Ultimately, one must admit, to himself foremost, that planning and strategizing is as important as being truthful and moral. There's no sin in weighing your options, being wise, and looking after yourself in the face of danger.

CHAPTER 9: BLACK PANTHERS

In the aftermath of Malcolm's death, numerous Black nationalist organizations were founded based on his teachings, with the purpose of resisting police brutality. Founded in 1966, the Black Panther Party was one of these organizations. The Black Panthers were established by Bobby Seale and Huey Newton, whose intention was to challenge police brutality against African Americans. Panthers wore black leather jackets and berets, and they organized citizen patrols across numerous US cities. The organization peaked with around 2000 members in 1968 and soon fell apart due to armed conflict with the FBI, internal rivalry, and counterintelligence activities (Cleaver & Katsiaficas 2014).

The History of the Black Panthers

The founders of the Black Panthers, Bobby Seale and Huey Newton, met as students in Oakland, California at Merritt University. They joined forces to protest the college's Pioneer Day celebration. The celebration honored California's first settlers but left out the significance of African Americans in settling new lands. They later founded an organization that advocated for including Black history, and the contribution of African Americans to important historic events. The organization was called the Negro History Fact Group, and it raised awareness for schools to offer Black history classes.

The two men had a history of anti-racist activism, and

the tragic shooting of an unarmed Black teen Mathew Johnson soon after Malcolm's assassination drove them to establish an organization that would fight police brutality. The organization's original title was "The Black Panther Party for Self-Defense", and its members monitored police activities in Black communities across the US. The Panthers gained more and more popularity as they became politically active and had started multiple social programs. They also had support from Black communities in Philadelphia, New York, Chicago, and Los Angeles. The more they grew, the more the Panthers became a concern for the FBI.

The Panthers were often accused of being a gang, but their activities revolved more around social activism and politics. The group focused on Black pride, civil rights, and community control. They developed a program that consisted of ten points for ending police brutality, justice for all African Americans, housing, land, and better employment of Black Americans. The party was based on the Marxist ideology, which shaped their political goals and philosophical views.

Still, they were seen as a potential threat. The party itself sought more African Americans to be included in politics and elected for office. They didn't find much success in this area, and the FBI used counterintelligence to weaken the organization by stirring conflict among the members. This weakened the Party's political influence and served to harm their image. Although often slandered in the media, Black Panthers established multiple social programs that helped improve the position of African Americans across the country. They started free breakfast programs in schools and established free health clinics in a dozen of African American communities countrywide.

Despite the group's devotion to social work, scandal soon followed. One of the Panthers' leaders and founders, Huey Newton, allegedly shot John Frey, an Oakland police officer in 1967. Newton was charged and sentenced to up to 15 years in prison, but the decision was later reversed by an appellate court. However, this wasn't the only incident that involved the members of the Panthers.

The organization also had its own newspaper, which was founded by Bobby Hutton, then only 17 years old. Hutton, and Eldridge Cleaver, who was the editor of the newspaper, were involved in a shooting with the police. The incident happened in 1968, and two police officers were wounded in the shootout. The Party wasn't only encountering problems with the police forms. Internal conflicts were frequent, and it wasn't unusual for them to become violent. A major incident occurred in 1969 when a member of the Party, Alex Rackley, was accused of being a police informant. Several other members of the Panthers tortured and murdered Rackley, and Betty Van Patter, a bookkeeper who was a member of the Party, was murdered in 1974. The Party's leaders were thought to be behind the killings, but the crimes remained unsolved.

The Black Panthers were thought to be a threat to national security, so the FBI created COINTELPRO, a counterintelligence program, to keep track of the Panther's activities and whereabouts, and to stir conflict within the organization. The FBI declared the Panthers to be a communist organization that posed a threat to the entire country. J. Edgar Hoover, the first FBI director, even named the Panthers one of the biggest threats to US internal security. The FBI was said to have been exploiting the already existing conflicts within the Panther's ranks to further drive a wedge between its members. The conflicts would then serve to discredit the organization in the eyes of the public, which, in return, would weaken their influence. However, whether intentionally or not, these events undermined the Free Breakfast program and other programs that the Black Panthers had instituted. Accusations were made that the FBI was trying to dismantle this program, as to keep the Panthers from further establishing their authority.

Furthermore, suspicions at the time were that the FBI would engage in exploiting the rivalry between different nationalist groups, likewise, to undermine their influence on the public. Arguably, there's insufficient evidence to confidently state that such activities actually happened, and to name the exact parties involved in the said events. However, given that the journalist's investigation into the murder of Malcolm X revealed that intelligence played a major role in fueling the conflicts that resulted in his death, the assumptions don't seem to be far-fetched. Considering that the decades that followed showed that there was no real threat coming from a multitude of African American organizations, both passive and proactive, one can conclude that the paranoia and accusations made of the activities of these organizations were also exaggerated. Time has shown that neither the Black leaders nor the religions and philosophies that they were propagating had the goal of undermining the state security in any way. Quite the opposite, it is police brutality and the lack of ability to control crime without resorting to abuse of power that remain a struggle to this day.

In 1969, another incident sparked the Party's outrage, as two of their members, Mark Clark and Fred Hampton were shot while sleeping in their apartment. Although the police stated that the shooting, and consequential killing of the members, was a result of an armed conflict, the ballistic evidence that was later revealed proved otherwise. The evidence showed that the Panthers fired a single bullet out of the hundred that were found at the scene. The role of the FBI in this instance remained unresolved as well. However, a federal grand jury found that, while they weren't directly responsible for the raid, they had a role in the events that led up to it. Under the pressure of the scandals that followed them, increased by the severity of the conflicts that were happening within the Party itself, the Panthers officially collapsed in 1982.

The Black Panthers are called many names. Depending on who you ask, they can be seen as a pro-social organization that worked for the benefit of the Black community. At the time, they were also seen as a hate group, accused of stirring conflict between the White and the Black portions of society. The Black Panthers were one of the many groups that have centered around African American rights, and their pro-social activities remain a legacy that should be respected.

What Can We Learn From the Black Panthers?

Judging by their philosophy and demands, it's easy to understand how the group could have been seen as a violent one. Indeed, some of the group's members had allowed violence to overcome their pro-social vision, and the consequences of their outbursts eventually led to the group's extinction. This diminished the potential that the group had, and overtook the positive goals they were building toward. Based on their example, we can draw out a couple of important lessons for anyone eager to engage in social activism:

Caution Is Key

As seen in both the examples of the Nation of Islam and the Black Panthers, violence is always to be avoided when establishing influential organizations. An organization may have positive intentions and values, but those who are allowed to join its ranks and represent it speak strongly about the types of behaviors that can be expected. Whenever a group is formed within a society, it can be seen as a potential threat if its narrative supports or advocates for any form of violent behavior —whether offensive or defensive. In the case of Black Panthers, their brushes with the law helped discredit the entire organization. Here, the importance of ethics, integrity, and reputation of those who partake in and represent organizations becomes extremely important.

Free Breakfast Programs

The Black Panthers left one permanent, important piece of legacy: their program that enabled children to have free breakfast at school. It seems as if, despite grand visions, it was the small, planned, organized, and concentrated efforts to aid a specific group of people that made the most impact. The group may have planned on changing the nation, but instead, it managed to make visible progress within the realistic scope of their means and abilities. Had the group remained focused on 'small' efforts such as these, it is questionable if they would have encountered such harsh judgment and criticism by the public. The free breakfast programs are present nationwide today as well and make a true difference for many underprivileged children.

Non-Profit Organization

The Black Panthers established several non-profit causes, which collected funds and granted them to those who were in need. The money was given to African Americans who needed help with schooling, clothing, and provided many other services. They also supported research on sickle cell anemia, which produced a lot of the knowledge that is valuable until this day.

The Intercommunal Institute

The Black Panthers founded the Intercommunal Institute, an organization that addressed teaching principles in public schools. They impacted how schools observed their own structure, and the Institute was active for almost 20 years.

Inclusive Policies

Many members of the Black Panthers remained in the office on both the federal and local levels. More than advocating for Black civil rights, this organization was supportive of the gay liberation movement. They observed homosexuals as an oppressed group as well and engaged in bettering their position in society. Huey Newton, the co-founder of the Party himself openly supported the gay liberation movement. The Party also supported the women's liberation movement, encouraging its members to examine their prejudice and biases against feminism and homosexuality.

If you were to judge based on the 1960s and 70s media, you would have been given a gruesome representation of the dangerously violent group of Black supremacists who worked to undermine the positive values of society. Much can be discussed regarding the reasons for that. Partially, it could have been because many of the revolutionary ideas were rising at the same time, and the organizations that advocated for them held the authorities directly responsible for injustice, oppression, and discrimination brought upon the members of various minority groups. However, as you can see, the paranoia was unfounded. The Black Panthers were accused of many things, but the good that they managed to do lives on. In many ways, modern-day human rights organizations suffer the same fate. Their members may not be persecuted, and they don't fear for their lives as severely as their predecessors. But, the public isn't eager to change. Communities set certain standards, beliefs, and morals because they are beneficial to them. They provide much-needed security, and shaking these beliefs is bound to face resistance. Point out injustice in a community, and you will be accused of having some form of malicious intent. However, providing help for those in need remains a cause all communities can agree on. The legacy of the Black Panthers concerned those in need, and it made a real difference. This is one of the main reasons why they are remembered until this day.

CHAPTER 10: VIEWS AND TRANSFORMATION

Malcolm eventually began to believe that the only solution for the oppression of non-White peoples is for them to unite and eliminate it completely. However, it is the intricacy of actions that this would imply that often sparks the ongoing dispute about whether or not Malcolm was an extremist. He remained an inspiration and a role model for many people of color who otherwise didn't believe in violence and extremism on the one hand, while on the other, many who do have these beliefs see him as an idol.

From the present day's point of view, it becomes clear that it is impossible to interpret Malcolm's work without looking into the culture surrounding the era. We must remember that the world he was talking about was a world of open, undisputed racial segregation and silent oppression. It won't be until multiple decades after his passing that proper legal, social, and economic tools are established for social justice and rebellion to be put to action in non-violent ways. We also need to consider the fact that people of color had very little economic support at the time, and that the social climate wasn't such as to nurture equality and well-being of each citizen, regardless of their race and ethnicity. We also need to remember that the prospect of violent rebellion still remains one of the ultimate tools of social justice when institutions fail, even in countries that are known for nurturing humane values, like Scandinavian countries and the countries of Western Europe (Rabaka, 2002).

Public Image and Rhetoric

Malcolm founded the organization "Muslim Mosque, Inc." using his celebrity status. The organization was founded in Harlem, and unlike some of his previous endeavors, and the Nation itself, it was more inclusive in admitting members. This organization was more focused on the economic and political independence of African Americans. However, instead of focusing on the new organization, Malcolm decided to make a pilgrimage journey to Mecca. Since he was currently cut off from using the Nation's funds, he obtained money from his sister, Ella.

Malcolm abandoned his street ways long before leaving

prison, but he still used some of his hustler skills in life when needed.

He often used the narrative to appeal to the masses and gain a reputation in the Nation of Islam. He relied on understanding his opponents, paying attention to his image, and always being on the lookout for anyone who may have wished to harm him. The use of these narratives earned him respect among his followers, and he didn't have much trust in anyone aside from his closest circle of friends and family.

However, the one time he abandoned these principles proved to be fatal for him. It was difficult for Malcolm to stop trusting Elijah, despite the scandal that broke and despite having found out that Elijah was trying to push him out of the Nation and have him executed. To a degree, Malcolm believed that although complex, the situation with Elijah could be improved. Their history was too much for Malcolm to completely write off Elijah, and the faith that he kept in his former mentor eventually came at a great cost.

However, Malcolm still used some of the skills gained in childhood to make way for himself in life. To protect himself from opponents and any danger they may have posed, Malcolm tried to understand the enemy's psychology and figure out strategies to instill fear in the public. One of the strategies he used was to understand how the police worked, in order to face their resistance the right way. One of the examples of this was when Malcolm foresaw the police actions that would follow, thanks to his hustler strategy to "study the enemy psychology." Malcolm designed a counterattack after a visit to Los Angeles newspapers.

Malcolm purposefully maintained his hustler image, despite having abandoned the criminal ways. His image was one of his obsessions, and he went to great lengths to defend it. One of the situations that shows how much Malcolm cared about his image was when he faced West Indian Archie in a duel, which was an experience that nearly got him killed. His reputation and tough exterior helped him deal with the public, and he wasn't afraid of dealing with any topics and answering questions to the White press. The press often accused him of provoking dangerous ideas and actions with his teachings, but Malcolm often relied on his manners and charm to turn the press and the public to his side.

Hustling to Empower

Malcolm's strategies and use of hustler tactics to sway the public to his side helped him prevent any harm from coming his way. He relied on his ability to understand the public and applied strategies for hustling individuals to hustle the public. This helped him advance in the Nation quickly and rise through the ranks thanks to his ability to contribute to growing the organization. His reputation and charm also contributed to him spreading his influence across Los Angeles, Philadelphia, Detroit, Harlem, and Boston.

His art of persuasion had a big influence on the power to recruit, which, combined with his understanding of street psychology and slang, made him much more persuasive to young Black people. However, despite his reputation and credibility, the public was mainly turned against him, mainly due to political, economic, social, and spiritual reasons. Malcolm advocated for ideas that were recognized as dangerous, but there was very little awareness in the public of what sort of aggression and mistreatment these ideas appear in response to. The notion that African Americans must show aggression to defend themselves may appear as violent on its own, but if we consider the amount of not only discrimination but also violence by authorities and racially motivated crimes that African Americans faced during this period of time, it's easier to understand how fighting back could be seen as the best way forward. Malcolm advocated for African Americans to be proactive in order to improve their social position, which aligned with Elijah's teachings to a certain degree.

CIVIL RIGHTS BY RESISTANCE

Many Black leaders of the time advocated for African American civil rights, but they differed in their views of how this fight should be carried out. These differences often led to conflicts between them, and such conflict arose between Malcolm and Elijah Muhammad as well. Elijah Muhammad had a vision for Black Americans to connect with their African roots and establish themselves as conservative members of the middle class. He chose a non-political path to spread his views. However, Malcolm was more interested in the problems of the poor and was driven by the ideas of Marcus

Garvey's pan-Africanism. Malcolm also took a political route, which didn't bode well with Elijah. Although both men advocated for economic and cultural separation and didn't approve of Black leaders who advocated for integration, the differences in their views often caused conflict between the two.

The differences in views on racial justice and methods to achieve it illustrates how complex the racial issue in the US was and remains to this day. The burning questions remain whether or not activism should be done in a peaceful and non-violent way, and many African Americans remain torn between integrating and staying connected to their roots. More importantly, this moral conundrum affects how racial equality is to be observed —whether it's a community that knows no race, in which all individuals are being viewed as the same regardless of cultural differences, or if this sort of leveling causes people to distance themselves from their cultural identities, causing minorities and Black communities to lose their cultural authenticity.

CHAPTER 11: MURDER

In 1959, Elijah Muhammad and Malcolm X agreed to write biographies. The project was started at the initiative of Alex Haley, who wrote two pieces about the Nation's leaders. Both Malcolm and Elijah took some convincing, but eventually agreed to have their life's work written down once they began to trust Haley and his publisher. It took Haley multiple interviews to gain Malcolm's trust since the prominent leader was otherwise suspicious of all reporters. The production of Malcolm's biography had a rocky start, since he would only use the Nation's rhetoric and was quite distant when it came to opening up about his experiences and personality. This made it more difficult for Haley to understand Malcolm. Haley obtained much valuable information from Malcolm's notes on various pieces of paper that contained his private thoughts and spoke a little bit more to his personality.

After having spent a lot of time with Haley, Malcolm began sharing more of his private experiences, and this was when the writing of his autobiography truly began. It happened to coincide with the fallout with Elijah Muhammad, and the final passages of the book were written by Haley since Malcolm was assassinated before finishing the book. The book contains detailed descriptions of death threats that Malcolm was receiving.

The Assassination

Malcolm X's death was swift and sudden. On January 21, 1965, Malcolm was giving a lecture at Harlem's Audubon Ballroom. Three members of the audience shot and killed Malcolm in the room which he had rented for the purposes of his organization. The police arrested the attackers, and they were later convicted. The suspicions still remain whether the plot within the Nation's highest ranks resulted in his assassination, or if there was a more powerful figure behind Malcolm's death. Some of Malcolm's past statements suggest that other individuals and organizations wanted him out of the way. Despite the conspiracy theories surrounding Malcolm's death, his teachings and legacy lived on.

People of all colors, religions, and social stances attended Malcolm's funeral. An Arab sheik from Mecca performed the funeral rites, which included an Islamic

HOW TO FIND FREEDOM AND KILL YOUR FEAR   109

view of what the spiritual life following the Day of Judgment looked like. This was symbolic of Malcolm's soul ascending to paradise. After Malcolm's passing, his biography/autobiography remained one of the most detailed resources that depicted his life and work. Considering the situation in which it was written and completed, it can be considered both a biography and an autobiography.

Another suspicion surrounding the records of Malcolm's life and work concerned Haley's scholarly integrity. Despite being one of the most prominent African American authors, his book *Roots* has been dismissed by critics as insufficiently researched. However, his work on Malcolm's autobiography was largely approved by the author before his passing. This gives it a little bit more credibility, but was still insufficient to prevent the debate of whether or not the book contained exclusively Malcolm's authentic thoughts. Some of the critics refer to the two men's close collaboration as a source of skewing the focus of the book from Malcolm's honest, authentic recollection to sharing what he wanted to teach others.

Some evidence to support this comes from notes Malcolm would spontaneously write down during interviews. These notes show that Malcolm didn't practice the rhetoric he was preaching publicly and that he was a lot more open-minded than it appeared. Some of his notes even express tolerance for Christian and

Jewish people alike during his earliest, most intense submission to the teachings of Elijah Muhammad. Malcolm expressed his perception of the complexity of hate and religion by stating that millions of Jewish lives would be preserved had Christianity been truly practiced in Germany.

Beneath the Surface

Malcolm's notes reveal that despite the proclaimed Nation's principles, Malcolm was generally concerned about prejudice among people, not just toward African Americans. These notes also show that Malcolm kept a great devotion to his innate belief system, even though they contradicted the Nation's. He deduced that silencing a man—referencing how Elijah silenced him after his controversial statement revolving around the Kennedy murder—doesn't mean truly converting him. The Nation's leader demanded that the organization's members remain quiet about the murder, and Malcolm's rebellion went straight against Elijah's wishes. In this situation, Malcolm showed that, regardless of his enormous loyalty to the Nation, he still maintained a lot of individuality. He never abandoned his true principles, and the thoughts that were revealed after his death suggest that he censored himself a lot of the time to remain loyal to the Nation's narrative.

. . .

The Mystery Unveiled

Malcolm's assassination is a known fact, but for long, the circumstances leading up to his death, and the culpability for it if not direct responsibility, has been widely discussed. Did Elijah Muhammad hire or send his assassins? If not, was it his indirect rage toward Malcolm that drove his followers to murder? Did authorities know that Malcolm was in grave danger, and if they did, did they do enough to protect him? Many questions are left unanswered, and although blatant and a seemingly simple case, the death of Malcolm X remained a mystery for decades after.

When Malcolm teased King during their only encounter that he would now too be investigated, he had his reasons for saying so. At the time, the Nation was considered a threat to public safety. Malcolm and other members of the Nation, including Elijah Muhammad himself, were being followed and their phones tapped. Their movements and activities were followed carefully, so the question imposes itself: How were the state police unaware of the fact that Malcolm's life was in danger, and wasn't it their duty to protect him? A journalist, Abdur-Rahman Muhammad, who was intrigued by the circumstances surrounding the murder for the majority of his adult life, answered these questions in a now-famous documentary series called *Who Killed Malcolm X?* In this series, Muhammad investigated rarely seen records and evidence that proved just how big the threat to Malcolm was. As it turned out, the FBI saw him as a greater threat than time had shown Malcolm to be. The FBI was alarmed by the prospect of two charismatic leaders unifying the Black nationalist movement.

The sequence of events that began with Malcolm's controversial statement on the President's death, which was thought to have enraged Elijah, was only a part of the bigger story, as shown in later findings. As it turned out, their conflict was further fueled under the influence of third parties, one of them being Edgar Hoover, who specialized in suppressing right-wing radicals. Hoover engaged in discrediting nationalist leaders, which prevented them from gaining responsibility. A lot had been done behind Malcolm's back to discredit him, which was further shown by an internal memo from the FBI. The New York Police Department was aware of the threats made to Malcolm's life but still didn't provide security for him. Further investigation revealed that Malcolm was offered security, albeit reluctantly. He refused it, and not much was done afterward to protect his life. The lack of interest in investigating his murder further was noticeable through a rushed investigation. The ballroom scene was cleared out within hours so that the facility could return to use as usual. Another hole in the investigation concerned the number of alleged assassins. According to many eyewitnesses, there were five gunmen, but the police narrowed down the suspect list to only three, without explaining this decision. This raised the question of why there wasn't further investigation into more possible conspirators.

Further investigation suggests that the FBI was familiar with the schism within the Nation, and had been exploiting it to undermine the influence of the organization. Stories that were circling the media seem to have been used to further fuel the conflict between the two men. There was a lot of paranoia surrounding the Nation, which can be reflected upon in the light of modern political circumstances. The fear that the organization might cause a nationwide conflict showed to drive a lot of violence and animosity toward its members, but the discovered materials showed that the allegations couldn't be further from the truth. Despite their strong rhetoric, the Nation didn't gather or possess significant weapons, nor had they created plans or set goals to intervene with politics. Quite the opposite,

Elijah Muhammad himself stood firmly in his intent to stay out of politics, perhaps to avoid accusations like these.

However, another significant element to the story was discovered that might better explain the animosity toward Malcolm. The Nation was in charge of substantial riches, and Elijah Muhammad himself did not indulge in the amount of luxury as to doubt his intents. But, his children were shown to have had a great interest in the Nation's funds, and had been some of Malcolm's greatest critics. Some of the latter findings suggest that Elijah's family felt threatened that Malcolm's popularity might draw followers away from the organization, hence depriving it of its income. One of the contributing motives to Malcolm's murder could have been financial, if not purely personal in nature. Combined with the informant's efforts to deepen the wedge between the two leaders, it's easy to see how flammable the situation was for a long time before the murder.

Another mystery concerned the physical description of the alleged murderer. Witnesses gave different descriptions of what the man who shot Malcolm looked like compared to the appearances of the men who were accused and sentenced for it. To neglect such important discrepancies is peculiar to say the least.

Last, but not least, numerous death threats that Malcolm began receiving after leaving the NOI,

HOW TO FIND FREEDOM AND KILL YOUR FEAR 115

followed by the fire-bombing of his house, were obvious signs that the danger was serious. The tensions seemed to have been grave with the so-called Fruit of Islam, which were the organization's young and impressionable members. The FBI feared that they could have been turned into a paramilitary force, so informants kept a close eye on their activities. Furthermore, some evidence appeared that there was a whisper campaign in the organization against Malcolm, although its instigators weren't openly suspected or mentioned. The campaign either altered or invented stories about what Malcolm said or did, which served to fuel the rage against him. Further journalist investigation revealed that Malcolm was surrounded by informants and that one of his closest and most trusted security workers was an NYPD informant.

All in all, the circumstances of Malcolm's murder aren't likely to be completely revealed any time soon. What remains certain is that paranoia served as fuel for a chain of events that would lead to the assassination. First, the paranoia surrounding the Nation and its intent caused authorities to induce possible conflicts to weaken its influence. Malcolm was a person of interest as well, and Elijah's fears, unfounded indeed, created a rift that didn't have to exist. Finally, it is considered that the Nation's narrative was ultimately to blame for the assassination. The most recent evidence points strongly toward the fact that an innocent man was convicted of the murder, and that the alleged killer named William

Bradley (later Al-Mustafa Shabazz) died before any conclusions could have been made. This leaves the murder shrouded in mystery, again, but now with a better understanding of individuals and circumstances involved in it.

CHAPTER 12: LEGACY

The childhood experiences of Malcolm Little formed an obsession with racial issues in the US. Malcolm X's obsession with racism started after his father's murder and the subtle destruction of his family by welfare agents that followed. His memories were of White people destroying both of his parents and despite some positive experiences he had in his life, they largely shaped his perception of race throughout his life. Although his anti-White attitudes developed gradually, they shaped his philosophy and were only abandoned once Malcolm learned about unsegregated countries of the Middle East.

Not to say that Malcolm didn't show potential early on. Despite trying to integrate into high school, being in a racist environment, and having negative experiences with teachers and classmates only deepened his own racist beliefs. The situation didn't change much despite his attempts to start fresh and change environments. Malcolm encountered only worse racial segregation when he moved to Boston. One can't help but notice that he was growing up in a world in which he had no chance of winning. Had he given up on the idea of education, he would have justified the stereotype surrounding his race, and any attempts of education and fitting in seemed to have been doomed to failure. This is largely the reason why he couldn't picture a non-segregated future before actually witnessing it.

An Unlikely Transformation

The sequence of events that led Malcolm to prison began in Detroit, where he lived in a setting that painted the picture of hardships that followed those living in the ghetto and the manner in which they led to moral decay. Malcolm was quick to sink into drugs, gambling, and hustler ways, which only goes to show how tempting nightlife can be. This was the period when Malcolm learned how to manage on his own, learning about his enemies and mastering the art of building a reputation. This was also when he learned not to trust people and to use charm to manipulate for his own gain. But, this was also the point that led to his temporary downfall.

His temper and solitude earned him the nickname 'Satan' in prison, but once Malcolm opened up to other inmates and began learning, he proved himself to be anything but. The transformation he underwent during seven years spent in prison was truly an inspirational one, and it goes to show that a young man or a woman from the street can flourish and reach their potential if given the possibility. In prison, Malcolm found what he had arguably been missing all of his life. He first finds a mentor to model after, who is a source of positive attention and acceptance for Malcolm. Given how little positive attention he actually received since he lost both of his parents early on, it's not difficult to understand that the influence of someone willing to give him support quickly motivated learning, discipline, and education. Prison is often the place where inmates learn the value of a regular, healthy lifestyle, and it's not a necessarily tragic experience for everyone. Malcolm's prison experience set the foundation for his further growth and development since he left the prison a truly reformed man.

A Role Model

Malcolm first encountered the Nation of Islam in prison, where his submission to a moral authority truly began. This is where he started following the principles of Islam and devoted himself to personal growth and education.

Once he became a leader, Malcolm rounded a journey from a life of suffering through crime, addiction, and vice to a fully formed media personality, with credibility and shaped confidence. His personality was enhanced with the fully formed identity of a religious leader, which helped him rise through the Nation's ranks and even surpass his mentor Elijah Muhammad. He began getting more and more attention from the press, which allowed him to share his philosophies first within the bounds of the Nation's philosophy, and then wider until he eventually began addressing further social and political issues. Over the years, he managed to shape his public identity and persona and established himself as a relevant figure when it came to social and racial discussions both in the US and worldwide.

AN OPEN MIND

His openness to changing attitudes when encountering different experiences is considered to be the staple personality trait that first enabled his transformation from a criminal to a pious, religious man, and later from a leader into an authority figure. Integrity and modesty remained as his most prominent personality traits that produced such vast influence beyond US borders. Malcolm did appreciate and enjoyed luxuries and hospitality that were shown to him but never sought to accumulate private possessions or grow riches. Knowing that his words didn't come with ulterior motives, people listened to him and believed the things that he said. Based on that, countless people of color began considering themselves as equals, first striving toward segregation, and then visioning and eventually creating the still-evolving color-blind civilization that we know today.

Integrity is a signature trait of every effective leader, and Malcolm had and showed with each of his words and actions that he was thinking of the needs of people, mainly his own kin, and little if at all about himself. The ability to put other people's interests ahead of their own

HOW TO FIND FREEDOM AND KILL YOUR FEAR 123

is also a prominent leadership trait, and Malcolm demonstrated it with his actions.

Constant growth and change are something many struggles with, mainly because it is difficult to accept any sort of change, let alone when it comes to one's own views. After his pilgrimage to Mecca and experiences with Middle Eastern nations, Malcolm learned the true extent and power of Islam. He learned that the religion included many nations and races, and that at its core, it was tolerant and inclusive. This was where his views began to shift and he eventually abandoned his extremist views. Although the Nation thought of this change as a betrayal in a way, it actually led to more White people being included in anti-racist activism, unveiling the struggles of other non-White and non-American groups, and overall had an important role in creating a vision of equality. Earlier in the book, I stressed a couple of times that African Americans of the time weren't yet introduced to the concept of racial equality, and practically none of them had ever experienced it. One of the reasons why segregation was the first philosophy they accepted was that they had never even pondered upon the possibility of a racially undivided society. This sort of isolation closed many doors to growth and education, as high education and business success were given a 'White' etiquette, leaving African Americans with very few options in life, which only worsened their circumstances.

Malcolm's eventual acceptance of integration was

important because it inspired people to envision a life with no bounds. Before, he would have been exposed to three philosophies: either integrate in the US and abandon their racial identity, segregate and create a separate state for only Black people, or go back to their roots in Africa or the Middle East. The rhetoric that Malcolm offered with his maturing overview of race opened up, at least theoretically, an idea that each African American has the right to choose their own path. The 'color-blindness' that Malcolm witnessed during his journeys actually helped US Africans let go of the bounds of segregation and open up to working with White people to improve their position in society. Although these views are suspected to be the downfall of his relationship with the Nation, they were much more beneficial for his followers as they gave them further options in life.

We can learn many important lessons from this stage of Malcolm's life. First, one should gain as many experiences as possible to test and verify their attitudes and beliefs. Had Malcolm not decided to travel, he couldn't have learned about a way of living, unlike anything he had seen before. If one is to grow and prosper, learning isn't enough. Experience is necessary to broaden your horizons. His changing views on racial problems reflected his own personal growth, and there is another lesson for us to learn. Our earliest negative, defeating experiences may make us feel hopeless, powerless, and ultimately angry. We may feel hateful toward an environment and people who hurt us, but to let go of it is to grow. In Malcolm's case, embracing the idea of racial harmony didn't betray the memory of his family, nor did it diminish the tragedy and sacrifice of his parents. Instead, it helped him find peace, build his own family, and contribute to creating a community that would work to prevent tragedies like his from happening in the future. This leads us to think about how to process early triggers that instill rage and hate in a growth-oriented way. While Malcolm was consumed by hate and desperation, he fell further and further into decay, until he ended up in prison. Letting go of that hate and channeling pain and loss into faith, giving it a true purpose, and using it to better yourself and others is the right way to go.

Malcolm's intolerance toward White people was completely understandable, but it cost him a lot. He believed that Black people should never accept help from White people which, as we know, didn't bring him anything good. The decades to come transformed the beliefs of many White people, and they used both intellectual and material resources to contribute to positive changes in society. Unity instead of division is proven to yield true growth and progress for both Black and White communities.

CONCLUSION

It has been over 50 years since the killing of Malcolm X. Perhaps, enough time has passed for the individuals with valuable insights into his life to reveal things that the public was unaware of.

In this book, you learned the life path of Malcolm X. You learned that he had a difficult childhood, to say the least. From the modern-day point of view, it is hard to process that a family can be so cruelly persecuted for just sharing what they believe in. But, Malcolm grew up in a different society. It was the society that let him down, showing complete disregard for the lives and the well-being of him and his family. Malcolm's misfortune didn't end with the loss of his family. As you learned, he was an exceptionally bright child. Despite all odds, he was at the top of his class and was even selected to be a class president. But, there Malcolm encountered the worst form of discrimination a child could. He was made to believe that, despite his talents and hard work, he would never fulfill his ambitions to become a lawyer solely because of the color of his skin. Being told that your fate is to live beneath your true ability just because the community won't accept you for who you are would have been damaging to any child, and for Malcolm, it sparked a belief that he was surrounded by enemies. It instilled a nihilist philosophy that made him think that he could expect very little from life, and he acted like his life was truly worth very little. Before choosing to fight for African American political and civil rights, Malcolm was first a criminal. But, being imprisoned was a life-changing experience for Malcolm. In prison, he discovered an insatiable thirst for knowledge, and with a little bit of support, he found one essential thing that a human being needs to thrive: He found a purpose.

In this book, you also learned how Malcolm X shaped his views. You learned that early trauma made him a Black nationalist, and based on his traumatic experiences with the White community, he was quick to adopt the views of Black racism. In the early days of his membership in the Nation of Islam, Malcolm believed that White man was the Devil sent to torture African Americans and that the fight was the only true way to liberation from the oppressors. He maintained his philosophy almost until the end of his life, but he used his voice for good. No one could say that he advocated for violence, as he'd clearly stated that he stood for defense. Yet, the press was eager to discredit him. His views and words were skewed, and the press took every opportunity to make him look like a villain. But, despite the negative campaign, Malcolm gave hundreds of thousands of young African Americans a sense of direction and purpose.

Malcolm preached that prosperous life requires discipline, morals, integrity, and strength—all of which are now being preached by thousands of motivational speakers to anyone who will listen. Malcolm helped African Americans of the time find support and purpose. His vision was to empower those who were stripped of self-esteem and he gave people tools to build themselves up by understanding their value. Malcolm's philosophy was that of separatism, which he explained was a way for African Americans to assume their rightful place in society.

Malcolm held a strong faith in his mentor, Elijah Muhammad. While Malcolm gave his best to serve the Nation any way he could, the mistrust in him grew. Those he served believed he wanted to overthrow them. We now know that it wasn't the case, but little could be done to help Malcolm. As his influence grew, he was shunned from a community he helped establish.

Malcolm's faith was shaken to the core, and his pilgrimage helped him realize things he wasn't aware of before. First, Malcolm learned how the teachings of true Islam differed from the Nation's principles, which helped him grow spiritually and enriched his outlook on life. He experienced being in diverse cultures, and as someone who had never lived in a non-racist society before, he learned that there was, in fact, a possibility for races and ethnicities to live together and unite in their fight for the common good. He returned from his hajj pilgrimage a changed man, but this change didn't sit well with his mentor.

In this book, you also learned about how and why Malcolm X died. You learned that, on the surface, he had fallen out with the Nation for abandoning their philosophy, for exposing Elijah Muhammad's indiscretions, and for speaking out on the Kennedy murder despite being told not to do it.

But, as you learned, below the surface, the stage was being set to take Malcolm down for months, or even years before his assassination. You learned that Elijah Muhammad started mistrusting him because of his rising fame and that there was a whisper campaign spreading false statements between Malcolm and Elijah. You also learned that the Nation's leaders were being investigated by the FBI and that there was a clear pattern of authorities driving a wedge between him and Elijah. Lastly, you learned that Malcolm died mainly for displeasing Elijah, but also because their conflict was being impacted by third parties.

In this book, you also learned that Malcolm's legacy lives on. He was an enormous influence on African

Americans, who helped them see beyond the limitations of their society. Malcolm and his fellow Black leaders assured African Americans that they deserve human, civil, and political rights. They helped them rise from their oppressed position and pursue improvement and success.

HELP OTHER READERS TO DISCOVER THIS BOOK

P lease take a minute and write your <u>honest</u> about this book on the Amazon page.

Reviews are the life blood of the books, so I highly appreciate your time and your thoughts on what you got from reading.

Thanks a lot!

REFERENCES

Carson, C. (2005). *The Unfinished Dialogue of Martin Luther King, Jr. and Malcolm X*. OAH Magazine of History, 19(1), 22-26.

Cleaver, K., & Katsiaficas, G. (2014). *Liberation, imagination and the Black Panther Party: A new look at the Black Panthers and their legacy*. Routledge.

DeCaro, L. A. (1996). *On the side of my people: A religious life of Malcolm X*. NYU Press.

Dretzin, Rachel and Phil Bertelsen, directors. *Who Killed Malcolm X?* Netflix, 2020, www.netflix.com/title/80217478.

Ezra, M. (2016). *Blood Brothers: The Fatal Friendship between Muhammad Ali and Malcolm X*.

Goldman, P. L. (1979). *The death and life of Malcolm X*. University of Illinois Press.

Rabaka, R. (2002). *Malcolm X and/as critical theory: Philosophy, radical politics, and the African American search for social justice.* Journal of Black Studies, 33(2), 145-165.

X., Malcolm. (2015). *The autobiography of Malcolm X.* Ballantine Books.

All images sourced from Pixabay.com

Made in the USA
Las Vegas, NV
10 March 2022